Joe Camp's Benji™
Off the Leash!

For Kathleen,
whose love and inspiration nurtured this story from start to finish

HarperCollins®, ☕®, HarperFestival®, and HarperKidsEntertainment™
are trademarks of HarperCollins Publishers Inc.
Benji: Off the Leash!
© 2004 Benji Returns LLC
Printed in the U.S.A. All Rights Reserved.
For information address HarperCollins Children's Books, a division of HarperCollins Publishers,
1350 Avenue of the Americas, New York, NY 10019.
Library of Congress catalog card number: 2004102991
www.harperchildrens.com
1 2 3 4 5 6 7 8 9 10
❖
First Edition

Joe Camp's Benji™
Off the Leash!

by JOE CAMP

HarperKidsEntertainment
An Imprint of HarperCollins*Publishers*

Preface

My wife, Kathleen, and I were with the new Benji in New York for an appearance on *Good Morning America*, just weeks after we had adopted her from an animal shelter in Gulfport, Mississippi. We checked into the hotel in midtown Manhattan, took Benji for a walk, gave her a good meal, and prepared to head out for a nice dinner ourselves. There are probably more terrific restaurants per city block in New York than anywhere else in the world. On the plane we had spent at least an hour narrowing the long list and, during the taxi ride into the city, we had called on our cell phone and made reservations at our selected restaurant with anxious anticipation. But the anticipation was as far as it went. We never made it out the door. Benji refused to be left alone in the room. Absolutely refused. Would have no part of it. And she let the entire hotel know exactly how she felt about it. She had been abandoned once and wasn't about to let it happen again, thank you very much. So, it would be room service for us that night. As we ate our dinner, Benji was sprawled happily on the bed, very pleased with herself . . . and we began to wonder what she might've been through when she was out on the streets. Why would anyone abandon such an amazing dog? How long might she have been lost and alone before she was picked up, brought to the Humane Society of South Mississippi, and adopted by us to become the new Benji? At the time, we were planning a Christmas movie for Benji's return. But what bubbled up out of our experience that night in New York changed all that. We talked on and on, into the wee hours, about a dog abandoned, on the streets, having to figure it all out on her own. The result is the would've-been . . . well . . . could've-been . . . okay, might've-been story of the new Benji. We, of course, don't know for sure what happened to this bright, loving, beautiful dog of ours before she was adopted, but it could've been the story you're about to read. I hope you enjoy.

–Joe Camp

Foreword

The character Benji has always been male. Doesn't have to be, I suppose. It's just always been that way. The current dog playing the role is female, as was the second Benji. I learned long ago that bad things happen any time a male denies a female her birthright. So, I say loud and clear that the best two Benjis we've ever had have been female: the second Benji and the current Benji. And whenever I refer to the actual dog, which lies at my feet as I write this, and whose real name is Benji, I always refer to her . . . as a her. In deference to history, however, the character in movies and books will continue to be referred to as a he. Yes, I know it sounds crazy, but so be it. If I weren't crazy I wouldn't be in this silly business.

–Joe Camp

1

The heat was thick and wet all around him but Colby pressed on, peddling his bike through the narrow oak-lined streets of the little Mississippi town. A boy on a mission. Strapped to the front carrier was a worn canvas backpack—army green and past its prime.

Colby was late, and it worried him. Getting out of the house had taken way too much time. It seemed like his dad would never leave.

His dad.

Funny, he thought. In all his fourteen years he had never called him "Dad." Never even referred to him as Dad. Hatchett is what everybody in town called him. Just his last name. But Colby rarely called him anything. He often wondered how nature could get so screwed up as to create a father and son so different.

He slowed to a stop at Main Street, making a point of checking traffic both ways, not so much for safety, because there were very few cars on the street. It was mainly for the sake of Deputy Ozzie whose squad car he had pulled up beside. The deputy was talking on his cell phone and nodded at Colby without missing a word. Colby stretched to look beyond the car . . . and there it was, coming straight at him. His dad's green pickup.

He scooted back quickly and hunched low, putting Ozzie's car between himself and the pickup. It seemed to work. The truck passed without incident. Hatchett didn't see him. Ozzie eyed him curiously, and Colby moved on before the deputy could ask any questions.

He turned left and peddled up Main, through the park, and then turned left again onto Burton Street. Gulfport was a beautiful little town with a long history and no intention of giving in to the pace of today. Colby liked that. He wasn't a fan of all the rattle of the twenty-first century. Colby didn't watch television. Ever. He read constantly, losing himself in adventure tales like *Moby-Dick* and *The Golden Compass*.

He paused on the sidewalk before a withered and crumbling old two-story home, once an impressive mansion but now up to its porches in weeds. Bushes and shrubs, allowed to grow out of control for years, seemed to shroud the home in shadows. Windowpanes were missing, and a shutter hung broken from a bottom hinge. It was the kind of place that caused local kids to cross to the other side of the street. But not Colby. He glanced at an upstairs window, then checked behind him, down the street.

Drat!

It was the doofus brothers turning the corner in their weird orange van. They were actually not brothers, and doofus wasn't their name. That was what the kids called them. Because, well, because they were doofus-y. Always making mountains out of molehills. Taking themselves way too seriously. You'd think they were federal agents or something. But they weren't. They were dogcatchers. And now they were headed down the street straight toward him.

Colby peddled off the curb and pretended to meander down the street.

Livingston and Sheldon—their real names—slowed the van as they passed Colby, eyeing him suspiciously. They eyed everything suspiciously. Colby nodded, and they drove on.

When the van had turned the corner, Colby whipped around and peddled hard back to the old house. He dropped his bike behind a stand of bushes in the front yard, unsnapped his backpack, and raced inside.

Cobwebs and grayed sheets covered the sparse furnishings, but through thick layers of dust the exposed Victorian pieces reflected a splendor the house once knew. It had been a long time since anyone lived here. Colby took the stairs two at a time to the second floor and dashed into a tiny room overlooking the front yard. He jolted to a stop, and smiled warmly.

There, nestled on the hearth of a small, tiled fireplace was Daisy, a black Tibetan Terrier, and her five newborn puppies, squirming, squealing, and fighting for room to nurse. Four of the puppies were solid black, like their mother. But the fifth one wasn't black at all. Not even close. His coat was a weave of golds and reds and tan. The only black on this puppy was on the tips of his ears. Colby lifted the pup into the air and touched him nose-to-nose. "I'm different too," he said. "Don't worry about it. You're the cutest."

He returned the puppy to Daisy, then scratched the big black dog on her head. "How's it going, girl?" he said. "I brought you the good stuff this time. The canned stuff."

Colby withdrew a can from his backpack along with a glass bottle of water. He wrenched off the lid and gave the can a sniff. "Ugh." He groaned and rolled his eyes. "You're gonna love this."

Somewhere in the distance, the squeal of tires around a corner caught Daisy's attention. These were familiar tires. She struggled to get up but Colby, not realizing what was wrong, eased her back to the floor.

He should have listened to Daisy.

Outside, a green pickup truck passed the house slowly, obviously cruising, searching. Suddenly, it jolted to a stop and backed up. Hatchett got out and stomped toward the stand of bushes in the front yard. Colby's bicycle had caught his eye. He gawked at it for a moment, then marched toward the front door.

Colby had emptied the can of dog food into a plastic bowl and was pouring fresh water into another. He twisted the lid back onto the glass bottle. "Okay, take care now. Stay inside. No wandering about." Suddenly Hatchett stepped into the doorway behind him and bellowed.

"What's this?!"

He was a huge man, towering over Colby like a giant.

Colby spun around and the glass water bottle slipped from his hand, skidding across the floor toward the looming figure of his father. Hatchett slammed his foot into the bottle and sent it sailing across the room and smashing into pieces against an old radiator. Glass and water flew everywhere.

Colby stood up, his face ashen.

"You stole this dog from me!" Hatchett screeched.

"No, I didn't. She got loose, all on her own. I come here a lot and just happened to find her." The statement was only half true. When he found Daisy plodding down the country road near their house, looking for a safe place to have her puppies, Colby had led her to the old house. He had been worried about her because Hatchett was breeding her more than the book said was healthy.

"Don't give me that! She can't open the cage door by herself!"

"How would you know?" Colby shot back, because Hatchett never paid any attention to the dogs he was breeding except to count their puppies, and sell them. Hatchett pointed a warning finger at him and stalked toward the dogs on the floor.

"This is the most rare, the most expensive breeder I've got.

The only one in a six-county area! And look what's happened! She's gotten tied up with some mongrel and had mixed-breed puppies!" He jerked the golden pup off a teat and heartlessly tossed him aside. He slid, spinning across the dusty floor, all the way to the other side of the small room. Colby watched in anguish as the puppy picked itself up, none the worse for wear except for the raw fear in its eyes. The puppy just stood there, trembling, not knowing what to do next.

Hatchett picked up one of the black pups.

"These are probably mixed breed too!" he said. "Leastwise, they're black and look like their mama so I can probably sell 'em as pure!"

He spun around to Colby. "And I'm 'bout inclined to sell you too! Or something worse. Now pick up these pups and get your butt in the truck!"

Colby turned and started for the golden puppy.

"Did you hear what I said, boy?! Pick up these puppies!"

Colby could stand it no longer. He blurted "Did you forget that you slung one clear across the room?!"

"Not that one! I can't get anything for no mutt, so it ain't going on the payroll! Get the black ones!"

Colby's heart began to pound hard in his chest. "What's gonna happen to this one?"

"Not my concern," Hatchett said coldly. "Now move it." The huge man lifted Daisy off the floor and stalked toward the door.

"If you leave him here, he'll die," Colby pleaded.

Hatchett turned at the door and looked hard at the boy. "What's your point?" Then he spun around and clomped down the stairs.

Colby was near tears as he carefully lifted each of the four black puppies into the cradle of his arms. At the door he paused and looked back at the blond puppy, still trembling in the corner. The puppy turned and looked at Colby, scared and all alone. A tightness gripped at Colby's chest, and his eyes began to water. He vowed the puppy wouldn't be alone for long. Then he turned and walked down the stairs.

2

Colby plodded through his chores that evening, his heart aching, and his mind spinning. He had a plan, but for him it could be a dangerous one. It didn't matter, he thought. He would not leave that puppy in the old house to die.

He set out a dozen rusty dog food bowls on an old make-shift table in the backyard. Actually, it wasn't really a table, just two gray planks of wood, balanced on a couple of saw-horses. The bowls were grimy from use and needed to be replaced, but Colby knew that would never happen. Hatchett would never spend money on his dogs, much less time and effort. Across the long table were a dozen rickety, homemade cages, all occupied with unhappy dogs, some with puppies, some not. The only time any of the dogs got out was when Colby took them for a walk. They never got to run and play like normal dogs.

The cage bottoms were made of wire so that the droppings would pass right through. It was supposed to save time cleaning the cages, but Colby was certain that the wire hurt the dogs' feet. He lifted a big tub of dry dog food onto the table, filled a bowl, and walked over to Daisy's cage. He placed it inside and scratched her lovingly on the head. Her puppies were squealing.

He spun around at the sound of the screen door swinging open. Hatchett was staring at him.

"Hurry up and finish that and get upstairs to your room. No dinner for you tonight." Then he disappeared back into the house.

Colby latched Daisy's cage door and stood there for a long moment gazing at the empty back porch. He didn't like the word *hate*. He had been taught by his mother not to use it. But he couldn't help himself. That's exactly what he felt at the moment.

Later that night, after everyone was in bed and the house was dark, Colby reached out his second-floor bedroom window and tugged on a string that lifted the clothesline below off its hook. He pulled the line up and tied it securely to his bedpost. The other end was attached to a huge, sprawling oak tree down in the yard. He wrapped a small chain around the rope so he wouldn't burn his hands, and slid down the line to his bicycle, which was waiting for him at the base of the tree. Then, he was off down the street, pausing only long enough to make sure no one in the house had awakened.

He peddled feverishly across town, sticking as much to the darkness as the shadows would allow, until he reached the old house, which was even creepier by moonlight. But Colby didn't notice. He raced into the house, up the stairs, and into the little room where he had last seen the puppy, trembling in the corner.

But the corner was empty. Colby's flashlight skittered across the broken glass from the shattered water bottle and danced across the room.

Nothing. The puppy was nowhere to be found.

He darted into another room and looked under an old dusty bed. No puppy. He checked another room, then another. All empty. He sank in anguish onto the top step of the creaky old stairway. How far could a tiny puppy go?

A shutter outside, blown by the wind, squeaked on its hinges, and for a moment Colby thought it was something inside. Then there was another sound. Was it a whimper? He heard it again.

Yes! It was. Somewhere downstairs.

Colby raced down to the foyer and turned circles, listening . . . listening. There it was again. Coming from the parlor. He eased into the room, his flashlight darting from corner to corner.

Again, he heard the soft sound. Definitely a puppy. Where?

Over there. The fireplace. Behind the fire screen.

His flashlight climbed across the brass inlays decorating the fire screen and spread light onto the hearth behind it, and there he was. The blond puppy with the dark ears. Still trembling, but eyes bright, gazing up at Colby.

Woof.

Colby grinned. The word *cute* did not describe this dog. There was definitely something special about him. Something very special indeed.

A chorus of frogs was singing and the night air was cool as Colby trekked along the bank of the stream, the puppy tucked warmly inside his jacket. He was headed for his pride and joy. His secret pride and joy. His private fort.

The structure was almost invisible in the speckles of moonlight and shadow created by the forest trees. Logs, plywood, and corrugated metal, twisted and bent around two huge tree trunks, blended with green branches from an artificial Christmas tree and a stretch of old camouflage cloth, all made the fort seem to disappear into the surrounding woods. Were it not for the discolored door from a rusty old school bus built into the front wall, one might never know the fort was even there.

Colby reached inside the narrow peephole of a window and felt for the secret branch that, when pushed down, popped the door open. He went inside and pulled the door closed behind him.

Darkness. Pitch black. Then, suddenly, light from a lantern filled the small room. And an ungodly screech!

Arwaakkk!

It was Merlin, a scruffy white cockatoo Colby had rescued

from an animal shelter. His job was to guard the fort. And scare the dickens out of anyone who suddenly woke him out of a sound sleep.

The inside of the fort was as unique as the outside. It was an amazing assemblage of junk ingeniously strung together to make a shelter that was cozy, safe, and functional. Colby shushed Merlin. "Merlin, hush. This is a puppy. You're going to have to watch after him."

"*Uhh, ohhh,*" said Merlin with a squawk. He was perched on a limb of a tree that was growing right up through the middle of the fort. Nailed onto the trunk of the tree were wooden steps leading upward to Colby's emergency escape hatch that looked for the world like something right off a submarine. Merlin peered down at the new arrival.

"*Uhh, ohhh,*" he squawked again.

Hanging under Merlin's limb was a hand-painted sign with the words: EARLY WARNING DEVICE.

Colby unrolled a sleeping bag that was wedged under his makeshift worktable. He fluffed it a bit and placed the puppy right in the middle of the softest part.

"This will be your home for a while," he said, scratching the puppy on the head. "Merlin will keep you company when I'm not around, and I'll try to dig up some things for you to play with."

Colby stood, looking around the fort.

"Ah," he said, spotting his water wheel. "First, I'll get you some water."

The water wheel was actually an old wheel rim from a small bicycle with a handle taped to it, making it easy to turn. A rope wrapped tightly around the wheel where a tire used to fit, and then disappeared through the wall of the fort into the night air outside. Tied to the rope were a number of aluminum cans. As Colby turned the wheel, the cans were drawn into the fort from the stream, slipped under the wheel, then over the top, dumping water into a trough made from half a tree trunk. Outside, the empty cans were routed over a similar wheel nailed to a tree growing out of the stream. As the cans were pulled over the wheel, and back under, they dipped into the stream and filled with water. It was a clever device that had taken almost two days to put together. When the water spilled into the trough, it ran down into a large dishpan very close to the sleeping bag where the puppy lay, and he promptly helped himself to a drink.

Next, Colby pounded the wall of the fort with his fist and a secret door popped open revealing all sorts of goodies: Rusty tools, some fishing gear, a big fluffy towel, some weathered boards of varying lengths, and a few old bricks. He used the boards and bricks to construct a pen for the puppy in one corner of the fort. Then he covered the dirt floor with the fluffy towel. When he finished, he stood up, almost cracking his head on the bamboo periscope dangling from the ceiling.

"Food!" he suddenly blurted. "You need food." Then he realized that the puppy wasn't even weaned yet. He couldn't eat real food. This was going to be more difficult than he had thought. But when he lifted the puppy into the pen and looked down at those big brown eyes peering up at him, he knew it was worth it.

"I hope you appreciate me," he said, popping open the front door. "Now you stay!" Then he dropped his voice into his best impersonation of Arnold Schwarzenegger. "I'll be back." And with that, he was gone, shutting the door tightly behind him.

"I'll be back. I'll be back," Merlin mimicked.

The puppy just sat for a long moment, gazing at the closed door. Finally, he stood on his wobbly hind legs and peered over the tall boards that were intended to keep him locked in the corner. Things looked better out there. Especially that big puffy sleeping bag under the table. It was much softer than the towel in his pen. With a look at Merlin, the puppy began pulling himself up, scratching and clawing, over the tall boards. Finally, with a plop, he tumbled to the floor.

"Uhh, ohhh!" screeched Merlin.

The puppy didn't notice. He trotted straight to the sleeping bag, sank down into the fluffy center, curled into a ball, and went to sleep.

Merlin gawked down at the sleeping pup and clucked his beak. This was not good. Not good at all.

The gate in Colby's backyard creaked open and Colby wished he had remembered to oil the hinges. He didn't want to wake anyone inside. He tiptoed over to Daisy's cage, slipped a rope around her neck, and helped her ease out onto the ground. Her four black puppies began squealing immediately and Colby hurried to get out of the backyard, praying they would go back to sleep before they woke Hatchett.

As Colby and Daisy approached the fort, walking down the path by the stream, Colby noticed that Daisy seemed to be walking strangely, slower than usual, not keeping up. He had read that it wasn't good for a mama dog to have puppies too often. And Daisy seemed to be pregnant most of the time.

Kerschnack!

Colby whipped around in a panic. He calmed down once he realized the noise had come from his own foot snapping a twig.

Inside the fort, the puppy popped up, wide awake. He had heard it too.

"Uhh, ohhh!" squawked Merlin. *"I'll be back!"* The bird could do a mean Schwarzenegger impression.

The puppy crawled off the sleeping bag and waddled across the fort to the pen Colby had built for him. He pulled himself up onto a brick, then over the tall boards, plopping back onto the towel just in the nick of time. The door swung open, and Colby and Daisy came in.

"Warf! Warf!" barked the puppy, and his little tail wagged ninety miles a minute. Dinner was at hand!

"What a good puppy," said Colby, pleased that he was still in his pen.

Merlin cackled with laughter, but Colby ignored him.

Daisy was happy too. She licked her puppy on the face.

"Kissy, kissy," squawked Merlin. *"Gross!"*

Colby glanced over his shoulder at the big fluffy bird. "Kissy, kissy?" he said. "Where'd you get that?" Every once in a while Merlin came out with something that made Colby wonder how much of his talking was mimicking and how much of it was real understanding.

"Let's get on with the feeding thing," Colby said, as he laid Daisy on the dirt floor of the fort and lifted puppy out of the pen. "It's way past my bedtime."

He didn't have to show the puppy what to do. The hungry pup immediately began filling himself with Daisy's warm milk.

"Okaaay," chirped Merlin.

Colby nodded.

"Yeah. Okay."

And, for just that moment in time, all seemed right with the world.

3

Birds were chirping and a distant rooster crowed as the sun peeked over the horizon the next morning. Several black-and-white dairy cows grazed lazily behind an old, weathered rail fence that ran along a narrow, dusty road to a farm, way out in the country. The road hadn't seen a car in days until a rusty old sedan came skidding around the bend, spreading dust everywhere.

The car slid to a stop near the grazing cows and the passenger door flew open. A dog was sitting on the seat right next to the driver, happy as a lark to be out for a ride. He was blondish, sort of reddish-tan, very shaggy, with a long crooked tail and several wiry hairs bending down in front of his eyes. The tongue dangling out of the side of his mouth seemed almost as long as the dog was tall.

"Get outta here," the driver barked, and he gave the dog an unsuspected shove right off the seat onto the hard dirt below.

"And don't come back neither," the driver growled as he

hit the gas and sped away leaving the dog in a cloud of dust.

The scraggly mutt watched the departing car until it disappeared over a hill, then he seemed to shake off the entire experience. He checked out his new surroundings and trotted quite happily up the road to where the cows were grazing. They were Holstein dairy cows, white with big black splotches all over them. The dog snorted and gave them a friendly bark. Then another.

Most of them simply ignored him. But one looked him right in the eye as if to say: *What? Did you want something?* Then she, too, turned away. But it didn't seem to bother this shaggy dog one bit. He trotted happily up the road, quite certain that this new circumstance would turn into some sort of exciting adventure. He wasn't far from wrong.

In the distance, rising over the same hill the car had disappeared behind, was a bright orange van. If the dog had been able to read the lettering on the side of the van, he would have realized that he should probably leave these guys alone. It was the Animal Control van! Dogcatchers!

One of the men, Sheldon, saw the shaggy mutt trotting up the dusty road, tail wagging seriously, and screeched at his partner, Livingston, "Stop the van!" Livingston slammed on the brakes, almost tossing Sheldon right through the front windshield.

"What?!"

"A stray!" bellowed Sheldon. "We gotta get him."

Livingston sighed. "We got more important business.

We're on the hunt. A major investigation, remember?"

"But it's our job! We gotta get him."

Sheldon was searching for the shaggy mutt in the rear-view mirror.

"Our job is bigger than one mutt," said Livingston, shifting the truck into gear. "You said you wanted to move up. The mutt can wait."

"Doesn't matter." Sheldon sighed. "He's gone."

Something caught Livingston's eye and he turned to look out his side window.

"No, he's not," he said.

The dog was gawking up at him, tail wagging, tongue dangling out of the side of his mouth. Sheldon leaned across to have a look.

"That is the longest tongue I have ever seen."

"Wait here," said Livingston. And he eased the door open and stepped out of the van.

"Come here, poochie woochie. Cute little bundle of fluff with a tongue long enough to be a lizard."

Lizard Tongue began to back away. *Oh boy! This is gonna be fun!*

Livingston stretched a hand out to scratch him on the head.

"Come here, you little lizard tongue."

But Lizard Tongue hopped playfully backward, just out of reach, and barked mischievously at the tall gangly man. Livingston took a step forward, then another.

Lizard Tongue stepped back toward the rear of the van, again just out of reach. *This is fun! Big man's gonna chase me. Come on, dude.*

On the other side of the van, Sheldon eased out and tiptoed toward the rear.

"Hang on a minute. I'll flank him," he said, just loud enough for Livingston to hear.

Sheldon peeked around the rear of the van and saw Lizard Tongue backing away from Livingston, right toward him. He grinned, more of a leer than a grin. He was quite certain he had this dog in his clutches. He took a step, hands out, ready to grab.

Crunch!

His foot hit some gravel.

Lizard Tongue turned. *Oh boy! There are two of them. Even more fun!*

Livingston approached from the front, Sheldon from the rear. The squeeze play! Closer and closer. The dog looked from one to the other, his tongue hanging out, his tail wagging a mile a minute. Suddenly, they both leaped for him at the same time, and just as suddenly, he was no longer there.

Kerwouch!

Two heads collided, and the dogcatchers dropped into the dust with a *thunk*.

Lizard Tongue turned playfully at the fence. That was fun! He threw his head back and barked.

War-war-waaarff!

Sheldon was trying to pull himself up. "That's it! He's mine!"

"I say forget him. We got bigger work," said Livingston, his head throbbing from the collision. Sheldon managed to get to his feet, wobbling, still dazed.

"Bigger work will have to wait," he grumbled, turning to eye Lizard Tongue with a menacing stare.

The dog barked again, and dove under the fence, frolicking off among the cows.

Sheldon followed, dropping to the ground and rolling under the fence. Livingston couldn't watch. He knew this was not going to turn out well. He dragged himself over to the van and just sat there in the dust, his back resting against the rear bumper.

Over in the pasture, Lizard Tongue was darting back and forth, in and out of a maze of Holstein legs. Every time Sheldon had a close shot at grabbing him, the wiry mutt would vanish behind one cow or under another. First this way, then that. The dog was having a terrific time. Sheldon wasn't.

Sheldon sneaked around one cow and worked his way between two others, then finally dropped to his knees to peek through the cows' legs. There was Lizard Tongue, gazing right back at him, not two feet away. Sheldon leapt after him, but once again the dog was too fast. The mutt darted away, spun back, then darted away again before coming to a stop. One of the biggest, fattest cows in the pasture was looking back over her shoulder, her big brown eyes fixed on Sheldon—on Sheldon's rear end to be exact, conveniently within range. A perfect target.

Sheldon glanced back just in time to see what was coming.

Kerthonk!

The cow's hoof sank into his behind!

"Yeeeowwww!"

Over by the van, Livingston grimaced, but didn't bother to look up. He simply pulled out his cell phone and dialed 911.

4

Colby was on the living room floor, his school books spread out on the coffee table, trying to concentrate on his homework. He wasn't getting much done. The conversation with his father had not been pretty, and now Hatchett was in his face. "Do you think you're as smart as me? Do you? Have you had my education? Have you been breeding dogs as long as I have? Huh?"

Colby met his stare head on.

"It doesn't take a rocket scientist to see she's sick."

Hatchett reached for Colby. "You little . . ."

But Colby's mom appeared out of nowhere and grabbed his arm.

"Stop it!"

"Don't worry, Mom," Colby said. "He wouldn't dare."

Colby knew why, and so did Hatchett. One more run-in with the authorities and he'd be toast.

"You got no respect," Hatchett seethed. "Neither of you."

Colby couldn't let it rest. He didn't like watching Daisy

get sicker and sicker. Or any of the other dogs for that matter. "I just think she should get well before you put her though another litter. The book says—"

But Hatchett cut him off.

"I don't care what the book says. The book's not paying my bills. Now get out there like I told you and walk that dog. Then put her in the cage with old Duke." He turned and stomped out of the room.

Claire Hatchett turned to her son, wanting so much to comfort him. Colby met her warm gaze, wondering for the millionth time why she stayed with such an awful man. He had come close to asking her many times, but never had. Maybe he should, he thought. After all, he was fourteen now. Plenty old enough to be asking important questions like that, especially when his own life was so wrapped up in the answers. He turned and watched Hatchett vanish through the door into the garage.

He finished his homework before going to the backyard. Homework came first. Not because anyone pressed him to do it, but because he didn't plan to grow up and breed dogs and clean out septic tanks for a living like Hatchett. He eased Daisy out of her cage. Her legs were wobbly, but she followed him dutifully. He was going to walk her all right, right out to the fort to see her puppy, who was now four months old.

As Colby and Daisy approached the fort, Colby began to sneak down the path ever so quietly. He eased back the burlap curtain that hung over the tiny window. When he pulled back the burlap, sure enough, the puppy was fast asleep on the sleeping bag under Colby's work table. Colby grinned. This was a game they had been playing for some time now.

Colby let the burlap flop back down over the window, and then spoke much louder than necessary.

"Gee, Daisy. Do you think we should drop in on your puppy?"

Inside, the puppy woke up with a start. He leaped off the sleeping bag and darted across the room, nimbly jumping the boards into the pen.

Merlin snorted at the silliness. *"Come in now,"* he squawked.

A moment later, the door swung open and Colby and Daisy entered the fort. When Colby saw the puppy in the pen, he grinned. Daisy went straight to her puppy and licked him in the face, just as she had always done, every time she had seen him.

"Kissy, kissy," said Merlin. *"Gross."*

"It's not gross." said Colby. "You're gross."

"Uhh, ohhh. Get rid of the bird," said Merlin. It was some-thing Merlin said anytime Colby seemed to be criticizing him. Colby figured Merlin had heard that phrase a lot before he was dumped at the Humane Society where Colby had found him.

Colby snatched the handles of his bamboo periscope and peered through the lens, made from an old telescope eyepiece

25

he had found in a Dumpster. That and a couple of mirrors was all it took to have a functioning periscope.

"Uhh, ohhh," said Merlin.

"All systems appear operational," said Colby, sounding every bit like a submarine commander.

"Uhh, ohhh!" said Merlin again.

"Full power. Perimeter is all clear."

"Uhh, ohhh!!" Merlin said, louder than before.

Suddenly the periscope jolted to a stop and swung back to . . . Hatchett! Standing outside the fence yelling for Colby.

Colby freaked. He screeched at Merlin, "Why didn't you warn me?!"

The bird squawked.

"Awrwack!"

Colby stopped and looked at him. If a bird could look angry, Merlin did. Colby remembered all the "Uhh, ohhhs."

"Oh," he said. "So you did."

He grabbed Daisy's rope and headed for the door.

"Sorry. Ring the bell next time."

"Too loud," squawked Merlin.

Colby turned at the door and looked the bird in the eye. "You wanna go back to the Humane Society?"

"Uhh, ohhh," squeaked Merlin.

"Yeah, well, don't be a butthead. No talking back." He turned and headed out the door.

"Don't be a butthead," mimicked Merlin.

Colby stopped in his tracks. At times like this, he wished he knew whether Merlin was just mimicking, or if this silly cockatoo was really messing with him. Merlin turned away and nibbled on a toenail, ignoring Colby completely. Just then, the puppy barked!

Can I go?

"No!" Colby said sternly. "You stay." He started down the front steps, then turned back. "You know the drill. Jump in, jump out, go to the sleeping bag, whatever." And with one more curious glance at Merlin, he slammed the door and was gone.

5

The leaves on the trees around Colby's fort were once again deep into the rich greens of summer. It had been almost a year since Colby had saved the little snuggly puppy from the old abandoned house. And, even though Colby sometimes still called him Puppy, he wasn't a puppy anymore. He was a beautiful full-grown dog with a thick coat woven with rusty reds and golds and tans, with just a touch of black on the tips of his ears and around his muzzle. He had the most penetrating big brown eyes Colby had ever seen. To Colby, he looked exactly like the dog Benji from the movies. Colby was too young to have seen the original Benji movies at the local theater, but he had seen some of them on television with his mom. So, as the puppy grew, he started calling him Benji.

Benji had learned to get in and out of the fort anytime he wanted, but it was his secret. At the moment, he was lying outside the fort with his chin on the ground, eyes on the path, waiting, wishing for Colby. It was well past the time when

Colby usually came. Finally, Benji made a decision.

At the house, Claire was making lunch for Colby and they were talking. Colby had long ago told his mom about Benji and he was trying to convince her that he should talk to Hatchett about bringing Benji to the house.

"No, you mustn't tell him," she said. "He'd make life miserable for you and the puppy."

"But he's not a puppy anymore. He's full-grown! I can't keep him locked up forever. Except when I walk him, he never gets out of that fort."

Colby would've been very surprised had he walked outside and looked off into the woods approaching the backyard, for there was Benji, trotting along happily, sniffing his way to Colby's house. He paused at the fence, glanced around, and decided to have a look at the house. It seemed big, much bigger than the fort. Somewhere back in his memory Benji could remember another house, even bigger. And dark. He could remember dark.

"As I said, don't irritate your father," Claire was saying. "We'll all be the worse for it."

Just then, Benji popped up in a window, peering in at Colby and Claire. They didn't see him, which was fine with Benji. Knowing Colby was okay was enough. Next came a familiar flapping sound, and suddenly Merlin was sitting on the windowsill next to Benji. Worried about his friend no doubt. The dog and bird glanced at each other, and as if each knew what the other was thinking, they took off, dog on the ground, bird just above, frolicking across the neighboring pasture. A most unusual couple.

Colby and his mom continued their talk, oblivious to the fact that Benji and Merlin were out exploring the world.

"How come you stay with him?" Colby asked his mom. "He doesn't love you."

The comment clearly stung Claire. Colby had never been so bold before.

"Two parents are better than one," she said, as she placed a sandwich in front of Colby. "Besides, we gotta eat."

"Mr. Paul down at the market keeps asking why you don't come back to work."

"And why don't I go to law school like I planned," said Claire. "Because my place is here looking after you."

"'Cause he won't let you," Colby said, turning around in his chair to face his mom. "Like I said, he doesn't love you. And he doesn't love me."

Claire looked at her son and tears began to well up in her eyes. Colby continued, "You don't treat folks you love like he treats us."

Just then, Hatchett slipped into the doorway behind Colby. He had been listening.

"Oh, you don't, do you?" he said snidely.

Colby spun around, heart pounding. Then a stern resolve enveloped him and he stared Hatchett right in the eyes. "No, you don't," he said quietly. And he slid out of his chair and walked out the back door.

"Don't you go out that door! Do you hear me?!"

But the screen door slammed shut behind Colby.

"Get back in here this minute!" screamed Hatchett. But to no avail. Colby was gone.

Claire heard the gate latch open and close, and wondered where Colby might be going. Hatchett was seething, but he did nothing.

A short time later, there was a rustling in the woods approaching the Hatchett backyard, but it wasn't Benji or Merlin. It was Sheldon and Livingston, sneaking from tree to tree and bush to bush, closer and closer to the house. They managed to reach the tall fence that surrounded the backyard without being spotted, but it wasn't because of their ability to sneak. It was because no one was looking. They darted around a nasty mud puddle where Hatchett had left a hose running, and Sheldon stacked a couple of wooden crates next to the fence. They climbed up to peer over.

"See," said Sheldon. "Look at this mess. Can you believe anyone would have these dogs cooped up like this? It's a crummy breeding factory is what it is. We gotta nail this guy!"

Livingston was scanning the cages in the backyard. They were rickety and dirty and too small for the dogs to move around much. But, unfortunately, none of that was against the law.

"I don't see any laws being broken," he said.

"Well, you know there are," said Sheldon. "We just gotta find them. We need a search warrant."

"Nobody's gonna give us a search warrant without just cause," said Livingston. "We'll have to catch him breaking a law."

"We need to be on this guy twenty-four-seven. Stuck to him like glue. Walking in his shoes. We need to pitch a tent right here." Sheldon turned to point to the ground behind him and almost choked at what he saw. There, right where he was pointing, was the dog from the cow pasture, tail wagging, tongue dangling. He barked that strange bark that was somewhere between a bark and a howl, as if to say, *Hi guys. Wanna play?*

Sheldon was gasping for breath, tugging on Livingston's arm, stuttering, "It's . . . it's . . . it's Lizard Tongue!"

Livingston spun around and grabbed Sheldon's mouth, jamming it shut. "Will you shut up!! We are trespassing! Do you want to get—" Suddenly he saw the dog.

"Oh, hello."

Sheldon was struggling to get loose from Livingston's grip. He wanted that dog and he wanted him now.

"Gotta get him," he screeched through Livingston's hand, and as he jerked to pull away from his grasp, he lost his balance on the crates. His feet flew out from under him, and so did one of the crates. Both dogcatchers went sailing. The shaggy dog waited until just the right moment to spin and dart away, leaving nothing but the nasty mud puddle to break their fall.

Splat!

Splat!

One after the other, they went facedown into the mud.

6

Colby approached the fort with Daisy, quietly as usual. He glanced behind him, just to make sure he wasn't being followed. The fort was his only refuge and he would hate for Hatchett to discover it. He eased up to the fort and slid the burlap curtain aside to see if Benji was under the table instead of inside the pen where he belonged. But he was neither in the pen, nor anywhere in the fort! Colby popped the latch and raced around to the front door. Sure enough, the fort was completely empty. No Benji. No Merlin. Where were they?

Not far away, just through the woods on a dusty country road, the ugly orange Animal Control van skidded to a stop.

"What?" said Livingston. "Why did you scream for me to stop?"

"It was him," said Sheldon, pointing out the window. "I saw him. He went that way."

"I think you're seeing things."

"No, I swear it. We gotta go after him. Come on!"

Sheldon reached for the door and Livingston grabbed his arm.

"If we go, we're going calmly and quietly, and with a plan. I'll get the tranquilizer gun."

A big smile spread across Sheldon's face. The tranquilizer gun. Yes!

Meanwhile, just through the woods, Colby sat in the fort, elbows on his knees, head in his hands, growing fearful that Benji and Merlin might be gone forever. Suddenly he heard a distant squawk and looked up just as Benji was climbing the three steps into the fort.

"Where have you been?"

But Benji saw Daisy and trotted across the tiny room for a nuzzle from his mom.

"Squawreech!" cried Merlin, flying into the fort. He landed on the rope hanging from an old ship's bell and flapped wildly, making the bell ring.

"And you! Where have you been?" said Colby, but Merlin continued to screech and flap, and the bell continued to ring.

"What's the matter with you?!" Colby lifted Merlin to his perch. "Have you gone nuts?"

Suddenly it hit him, a mere moment before he heard the voice.

"Have *you*?!" Hatchett was standing in the doorway, bending low because the opening was too short for him. He glanced around the fort.

"What is this? Is this yours? And what is Daisy doing out here?! And who is that?"

He was looking at Benji.

"It's that mixed-breed puppy, isn't it?"

Benji took a step backward into a corner. Then another. He was afraid of this man with the harsh voice. He remembered those cruel hands that had thrown him tumbling across a room so many months before.

"I should've done away with that mutt when it was born." Hatchett took a step toward Benji, but Colby leaped between them.

"You leave him alone!" screeched Colby, pushing hard against Hatchett's big chest. Hatchett grabbed Colby's arms to push him aside.

"Uhh, ohhh," squawked Merlin.

"Are we interrupting something?"

Livingston, the dogcatcher, was standing in the doorway with Sheldon. Hatchett immediately let go of Colby and tried to act as if nothing at all was wrong. Benji seized the moment and dashed right between Hatchett's legs and out the door. Sheldon spun around watching him race up the hill into the woods. Colby smiled in relief.

"Hey!" blurted Sheldon, turning back to Hatchett. "There's a leash law you know!"

"My property," sneered Hatchett.

"This is Mississippi Forestry land, sir," said Livingston.

Sheldon nodded as if he really knew.

"Well, pick nits," said Hatchett. "It adjoins my property."

Livingston eyed Daisy.

"This dog doesn't look too healthy," said Livingston. "She a breeder?"

"I don't breed."

Colby's mouth dropped open. Sheldon and Livingston looked at each other incredulously.

"Much," added Hatchett. "And not her."

That evoked a round of frozen gawks from everyone present. Colby could tell Hatchett was actually becoming uneasy.

"Just every once in a while," Hatchett muttered, almost under his breath.

Sheldon straightened his back and mustered every ounce of importance he could. "We know exactly how much you've been breeding, Mr. Hatchett, and we're watching you!"

"Watching you," chirped Merlin.

"Exactly," said Sheldon, without even noticing that he was including a bird in his conversation. "Watching you. We're going to be watching you every minute. Make just one mistake and you're ours."

Benji was watching the conversation from behind a bush high on the hill outside the fort. He turned and moped sadly away. The fort was his home. The only home he had ever known. And Colby and Merlin were the only friends he had ever known. What would he do now? Where would he go?

He wandered down the path toward Colby's house, the one Colby used when he came to the fort to feed him. Thinking of food brought up another problem. Benji had not eaten today.

Colby, of course, wasn't home, nor did anyone else seem to be. Benji wandered around the back fence and off into the woods. By the time he reached the outskirts of town, his sadness was overcome by hunger pangs. He sniffed around the back alley behind Mr. Paul's market where there were lots of trashcans and lots of interesting smells. He moved closer, pausing to scarf up a piece of bread that was on the ground. He was trying to figure out how to get inside one of the trashcans when the back door suddenly flew open.

"I'll be back in an hour, maybe sooner," said Dudley, a tall teenage boy coming out the door with two large grocery sacks. A long loaf of salami was poking out the top of one of the sacks. It looked good. Benji watched the salami as Dudley stuffed the bags into wire baskets on either side of the rear wheel of an aging green-and-white bicycle.

Plop.

The salami squeezed out of the sack and dropped to the ground, rolling straight toward Benji. He licked his chops. A reflex action. But it wasn't to be a meal for Benji. At least not yet. Dudley had seen it drop, and he snatched it off the ground, looked around to see if anyone was watching, then dusted it off and stuffed it right back into the grocery sack. By this time, Benji was practically hypnotized by that big chunk of meat. He followed it off around the corner as Dudley rode the bicycle away.

The little white house was perched at the top of a rolling knoll on a carpet of lush green grass, surrounded by sprawling shade trees. Dudley was on the front porch, a grocery sack under each arm, knocking on the screen door. The main door was open, but no one came.

"Mr. Finch?" Dudley called.

No response.

"Mr. Finch!" Dudley called louder.

Still no response. Dudley walked over to the big picture window through which he could see the living room and beyond that, the kitchen.

"Mr. Finch!" Dudley called, still louder. He walked back to the door and yelled again. Finally, he decided that Mr. Finch would not have gone far and left his front door open, so he carefully placed the two grocery sacks by the front door, then climbed on his bicycle and left, not knowing he was being watched from behind a bush near the edge of the woods.

Benji eased out from behind the bush to watch Dudley ride off across a little bridge spanning a small stream. Then he turned to the porch.

Lunch!

7

Mr. Finch was aghast. Stunned. Who could've done such a thing?

"Who's responsible for this?" he screamed off into the woods. Mr. Finch was old and crotchety, or at least seemed that way. He peered over his spectacles at a tiny stub of salami, skin dangling, most of it gone. Consumed.

"Show yourself right now!" he bellowed to no one in particular. "This is thievery. Stealing. No answer to life's problems! Repent and you will be forgiven. Ask and you will receive." He peered over his glasses out beyond the lawn, looking off into the trees. "Steal and you'll get your head blown off." And he picked up the grocery sacks and plodded into his little house grumbling, "Wrong. Wrong, wrong, wrong."

Moments later he was right back on the screen porch with a small bowl and a cooking pot. The bowl contained the remains of the salami, and the pot was filled to the brim with water. He placed both down on the wood planks of his porch, then scanned the distant trees.

"Might was well finish it off. I'm not eating after you, whoever you are," he said. Then he retreated back into the house.

The grass on the small hillside was tall and green, but it didn't hide the bright blue uniforms worn by Sheldon and Livingston. They were hiding, or trying to, lying on their backs at the crest of the hill. Livingston had his tranquilizer pistol at the ready, already loaded with a dart that would put whoever it hit to sleep almost instantly.

"Okay, he's right there, right?" said Livingston. "Just over the bunker?"

"Right," said Sheldon. "Just over the bunker." If someone were watching, they might have thought that there was a wanted criminal just over the hill. But it was only Lizard Tongue.

"In range of the tranq gun," confirmed Livingston.

"Not six feet away," said Sheldon. "These eyes don't lie."

"You're absolutely sure?"

"I told you. These eyes don't lie."

"Okay. Here goes." And with that, Livingston leaped to his feet and spun onto the top of the bunker, holding his tranquilizer gun in both hands as if he were some sort of commando.

Nothing. No Lizard Tongue in sight.

"He's not here."

Suddenly there was a bellowing scream from Sheldon. Livingston spun around to see the shaggy mutt not four feet away, almost nose-to-nose with his partner.

Livingston swung the pistol up to aim just as Sheldon catapulted himself down the hill toward Lizard Tongue. Too late!

Kerblam!

The pistol fired, but Lizard Tongue was gone. Sheldon hit the ground with a thud, the tranquilizer dart embedded in his rear end. He let out a loud yelp that slowly turned into a silly giggle. He rolled over with a big grin on his face.

"I'm thinking . . . hee, hee, hee . . . I'm thinking . . . you missed," he laughed, then drifted off into never-never land.

Livingston sighed heavily and looked at his smoking pistol.

"Maybe I did, maybe I didn't."

Benji was outside the fence, listening quietly to the voices in the backyard. Colby and his mom were laughing and talking as they filled bowls with dog food. They seemed to be having fun, just being alone.

"So what did he do then?" Claire asked.

"He just laughed and said, 'You're right, Colby, so everybody gets out ten minutes early!' And the class went nuts!"

"That's great. So you're a big hero."

"He's really nice," said Colby.

"Yeah," said Claire. "It takes a special kind of person to admit he's wrong."

There was a moment of silence as Colby thought about that. They both knew someone who never admitted he was wrong.

"Yeah. It does," he said, then turned with a bowl and walked to Daisy's cage.

Benji had discovered a large knothole in one of the planks of the fence and was peering in, watching Colby.

"So, what's happening in social studies?" Claire asked.

"India," said Colby. "Ancient India. I liked Greece better. Did you know that's where the Olympics started?"

"I did," said Claire.

Benji watched Colby reach for the latch on Daisy's cage and slide it open. She was lying on her side and did not look well. Just then, the phone rang.

"Be back in a minute," Claire said, and she hurried into the house.

Colby scratched Daisy lovingly on her head and placed the food bowl into her cage. Then he closed the latch. Benji watched. Lift and slide. He could do that. If he could just get inside the fence.

A loud noise interrupted his reverie. It was a pickup truck pulling into the driveway, just around the corner of the fence. A door slammed, and then he heard a voice. *That* voice.

"What's this bicycle doing in the driveway?!" yelled Hatchett.

Benji spun and raced off into the woods.

Later that afternoon, Mr. Finch peeked out onto his front porch. The bowl that had held the remains of the salami was now quite empty. Nothing left. He stepped out to the edge of the porch and hollered out to the forest.

"So! You don't even say thank you! What kind of upbringing is that? Don't you have any manners at all?"

He picked up the bowl, gazing into its emptiness.

"Shame on you! Do you hear me? Shame on you!"

Then, as he turned to go back inside, a warm smile stretched across his face. He was pleased that somewhere out there a friendship was in the making. And he was quite sure he would meet this friend in due time.

The screen door slapped shut behind him.

That night, with his belly quite full of salami, Benji made his way back through the woods toward the fort. He didn't expect anyone to be there, and he knew how to get in through the window. He longed for the comfort of his soft bed under Colby's worktable. There was no moon out this night and the forest and the fort seemed darker than usual. Benji glanced up at the window and walked around to the front door, just to be sure. He nudged it with his nose and scratched on it with a foot. Locked tight. No sign of life.

Merlin didn't even respond to his scratching.

He retraced his steps back to the window and climbed onto a stack of wooden crates to peer in. Merlin was not on his usual perch. It was dark, but a white cockatoo would not be difficult to see. Suddenly, from somewhere above:

Yeowack!

Merlin was right above him, pacing frantically on a tree limb, trying desperately to tell him something.

"Eeeyahh," the bird screeched, but before Benji could react, two large hands had him around the rib cage!

"Gotcha!"

It was Hatchett!

8

Benji yelped, then squirmed and growled, while Hatchett held him high in the air as he screamed at him. Merlin let out a screeching wail. Hatchett's eyes were glazed over and his breath was foul.

"You're mine now, you filthy mutt!"

Hatchett's grip was suffocating Benji and there was no choice but to break that grip. Benji lunged at Hatchett's neck, snapping wildly. Hatchett screamed as if his throat had been cut and let go of Benji before he realized that the dog hadn't so much as touched him. Meanwhile, Benji landed on all fours and was all the way to the top of the hill before Hatchett could even turn around.

"I'll be waiting for you!" Hatchett screamed wildly after the retreating dog.

He glanced up at Merlin, who returned his stare. Hatchett

turned and stalked away down the path, rubbing his neck where he thought he had been bitten.

"Butthead," mumbled Merlin, *almost* under his breath.

Hatchett spun around, seething, not believing his ears.

Merlin puffed his feathers and looked him right in the eye. *"Ah, ah, ah . . ."* The bird seemed to be saying, *You don't want any part of this beak.*

Hatchett gazed at him for a moment, then spun angrily and tromped off down the path.

High on the hill above the fort, Benji watched Hatchett walk away. He considered going back, but he could never sleep safely in the fort anymore. Hatchett might show up at any time. He wondered when he might see Merlin again. And Colby. It's a big and lonely world without the folks who love you. He turned and moped off into the woods, taking the path toward the little white house with the loud but nice man who put out food for him.

On this night, the bowl on the porch was full of cereal. Colby had brought some to the fort once and Benji had not cared for it much. But it was better than nothing. All the lights in the house were off, so Benji ate quietly, then headed toward town. It was an hour later when he found the old house. He was way too young to have remembered exactly where it was, but somehow he knew how to find it. It looked just the same as he remembered. Apparently, it was still abandoned because the front door was standing ajar. Benji nudged his way inside and went into the room with the fireplace, the room where Colby had found him with the flashlight on that night so long ago.

He curled up in a corner and closed his eyes. In less than a minute, he was fast asleep. It had been quite a day.

9

The sun was still low in the sky the next morning, but Mr. Finch was already out on the front porch tending to his many flowers and plants when Dudley showed up with a delivery of groceries.

"Morning, Mr. Finch. I got your delivery, bright and early, just like you said."

Mr. Finch turned from his gardening table. "It's not just like I said. Day's half gone." He peered over his spectacles at Dudley and issued a quotation. "'Those whose lives are spent in bed will never prosper it is said.'" He paused for a moment, then added, "Ebenezer Pane."

Dudley just nodded. He had no idea who Ebenezer Pane was.

"Yes, sir. Sorry."

Mr. Finch walked over and took the bag of groceries from Dudley. A bag of dog food was poking out the top of the sack.

"What's with the dog food?" Dudley asked. "Did you get a dog?"

Finch turned at the door.

"None of your concern. 'Mind your business, don't mind mine, only thence your star will shine.'" Again, he peered over his spectacles, with eyebrows raised, and he waited.

Dudley squirmed for a moment, then it hit him.

"Ebenezer Pane?" he questioned.

"You'll go far, son," said Mr. Finch, and he opened the screen door and started inside.

"Mr. Finch?"

He turned back to Dudley.

"Who is Ebenezer Pane? We haven't studied him in school."

Mr. Finch smiled.

"Of course not." He smiled. "I made him up." And with that, he disappeared into the house.

Dudley just gawked at the screen door for a long moment, wondering if Mr. Finch was from Mars.

Weeds.

Tall ones.

Lots of them. Some of them moving. Some of them moving a lot. Because Sheldon and Livingston were on their bellies, elbowing their way, commando-style, as if through the jungle. Livingston held up a hand and they both stopped, and listened. Then they were off again.

"All clear. Come on," said Livingston.

"Tell me again why I'm draggin' my belly through stickers and cockleburs."

"For the greater good. If we are going to nail this Hatchett guy, we have to catch him in the act!"

Sheldon nodded, then paused.

"The act of what?

Livingston peered over the top of Hatchett's backyard fence.

"Something illegal. Anything that doesn't pass muster."

Sheldon joined him. Again he nodded, then realized he had no clue what that meant.

"What's muster?"

Suddenly Livingston saw Hatchett out by the cages.

"Get down," he whispered. They both ducked behind the fence. Sheldon found a knothole and peered through. Hatchett was standing by a distant cage with his back to them struggling with something. As he turned, he glanced toward the house, then walked too casually toward the back gate. He was tying a cord around a small burlap sack.

Sheldon and Livingston huddled behind the fence and listened to Hatchett go out the gate, hoping he wasn't coming their way. He didn't. He marched off toward the woods.

"Where do you suppose he's going?" asked Sheldon.

"I don't know, but we've got to follow him. Take a look."

Sheldon crawled to the corner of the fence, peered around, and gasped! There, not one foot from his face was Lizard Tongue! Tail wagging, tongue dangling out of the side of his mouth as usual. He reached out and gave Sheldon a big sloppy lick on the nose. Sheldon flung himself back around the corner, heart pounding.

"It's him!"

"I know it's him," said Livingston. "Now move out. We've got to follow him."

Sheldon was shaking all over. He was sure he was having a nervous breakdown.

"Not that him. The other him!"

"What are you talking about?" said Livingston. "Will you move out before we lose him?"

"The dog him." He pointed toward the corner of the fence. "Right there. The dog. That miserable scum of a lizard-tongue dog!"

"Pull yourself together! We have bigger business than that dog!"

"Give me the tranq gun," said Sheldon. He held out his hand. Livingston was wearing it in a shoulder holster.

"I'll give it to you. The same place I gave it to you last time, now move out, soldier!"

Sheldon eased back around the corner, with Livingston peering over his shoulder.

Lizard Tongue wasn't anywhere in sight.

No sign. Gone. Sheldon merely blinked.

"He's the devil," he mumbled under his breath.

They hurried to catch up. Hatchett was marching through the woods, a man on a mission. The dogcatchers were sneaking from tree to bush to log, looking quite ridiculous actually, trying to stay with him and not be seen. Suddenly Hatchett stopped and listened. Had he heard them? They weren't very light on their feet. They dove so quickly off opposite sides of the path that Sheldon got a mouthful of leaves for the effort.

Hatchett listened for a moment and, amazing as it was, decided he hadn't heard anything after all, and he moved on. After a bit, the dogcatchers followed.

Not far away, Benji was fast asleep under a sort of lean-to created by nature when several trees had fallen pretty much in the same place. Over the years, pine needles had plugged the gaps between the logs and it was dark and cozy underneath. He hadn't slept much the night before at the old house. The winds whistling through the open windows, and the creaking of the old floorboards had kept him awake most of the night. But suddenly he awoke with a funny feeling that he was in danger. He looked off down the path into the woods. Then he heard the crack of a large twig and spun around. There, coming around the bend in the path, was Hatchett!

Benji scooted deeper into the darkness of the lean-to.

Hatchett walked right toward the lean-to, his boots crunching twigs not two feet from Benji's nose as he passed. But pass he did, continuing down the path deeper into the woods, the little burlap sack swinging by his side.

Benji eased forward a bit to peer out at Hatchett. He watched for a long moment, wondering, when suddenly the snap of a twig behind him made him spin around. It was Sheldon and Livingston, darting and dodging from tree to tree, playing spy. Benji ducked back under the lean-to and scooted deeper into the darkness. Like the feet before them, Sheldon's and Livingston's passed right in front of his nose. And they were gone off down the path.

Benji stretched out to see if anyone else was joining the parade. This was supposed to be a remote part of the woods where he could take a nap in peace! He eased out from under the lean-to for a look at the troop heading off into the woods . . . when he sensed again that he wasn't alone. He darted back under the lean-to, then stretched to see if someone else was coming. And sure enough there was.

A dog.

A weird, funny-looking dog with a bent tail and a long dangling tongue, trotted down the path, tail wagging wildly, pausing now and then to sniff the ground or watch a squirrel dart through the trees. He slipped behind a tree to relieve himself, then scratched up the leaves into a mighty fury and trotted on.

Benji eased farther back, deep into the darkness of the lean-to. This passerby was shorter than the others and had a better nose. But Lizard Tongue trotted right by without a clue that another dog was just a few feet away.

Hatchett marched out of the woods into a green meadow that lead to an embankment overlooking a meandering river.

He stood at the edge of the bank for quite some time, then glanced behind him . . . and tossed the little burlap sack into the river. It was obviously heavy, for it hit the water with a *kerthunksplash*.

"We saw that, Mr. Hatchett. Saw every bit of it."

Livingston lead the way out of the woods, Sheldon following. They marched straight up to Hatchett.

Hatchett was startled for a moment, but quickly recovered.

"I beg your pardon," he said.

"We saw exactly what you did," said Sheldon. And for that he received Livingston's elbow in his ribs.

"Shut up," said Livingston. Then he turned to Hatchett. "We saw exactly what you did."

"Hey look," said Hatchett, acting nicer than his usual self. "I'm sorry, okay. I'm not the type to litter, especially in this beautiful river, but I brought my lunch today and, well, I know it's not right, throwing trash in the river and all, but if you won't tell anyone, I promise not to do it again. Whaddaya say?"

To his credit, Livingston did not buy any of it. He stepped closer to Hatchett.

"It wasn't your lunch, Mr. Hatchett."

"No, it wasn't," Sheldon chimed in, pointing a finger at Hatchett.

Hatchett glanced from one to the other and then his eyes narrowed, no longer hiding the icy chill behind them. "Prove it," he said. Then he pushed by the two and strode off across the meadow into the woods.

"You gonna let him get away?" asked Sheldon.

"We got no proof."

"Let's find the sack," said Sheldon. "It's gotta be down there somewhere."

They turned and gazed down into the river, swirling, churning, racing to the sea. Livingston looked at Sheldon and swallowed what he'd really like to say. "Come on," he said instead. And he headed back for the woods, Sheldon following.

Lizard Tongue watched them go from behind a bush. He wanted to know what everyone was looking at on the bluff. So he trotted over and gazed down at the river.

Whoa!

It's really way down there. And it's water. He felt dizzy and sick and recoiled immediately. He just sat for a long moment, staring across at the far side, trying to shake it off. Then he turned to go . . . and there, out in the middle of the meadow, was Benji, who had been watching the goings-on, curious about why everyone was headed to the river.

Cool. A new friend. The shaggy mutt leaped to his feet, bent tail wagging, lizard tongue dangling.

Warf! Hi, guy!

Benji didn't respond. He had things to do, serious things.

Lizard Tongue loped over to Benji, danced a silly circle around him, then paused, face-to-face.

Warf! He dropped playfully down onto his forelegs. *Come on, guy! Let's play.*

Benji snorted once, then turned and trotted off. There was no time in Benji's plan for play. Lizard Tongue watched him go, confused. He didn't get it. So much for new friends.

Hatchett slung another beer bottle into a trash can already full to the brim. It smashed into tiny shards. He tromped across the backyard, turned on the hose, and began filling a lineup of water bowls, splashing more on the table than was going into the bowls. In the cages, puppies yelped and dogs barked. He picked up a bowl, walked over, and slung it into a cage, much of the water spilling to the ground.

Behind him, a pair of eyes were peering through the hole in the fence. Benji was watching Hatchett's every move. Especially the way the cage doors opened. Hatchett flipped up the latch on Daisy's cage and slid it to the right. Daisy wasn't well. She was lying on her side with ugly goop in and around her eyes. Benji watched closely as Hatchett closed the cage door and slid the latch to the left. Suddenly he heard something familiar. Too familiar.

Warf! War-war-warff!

There was only one dog who had a bark like that. Benji spun around to look outside the fence. Nothing there. Then he heard it again, along with a sort of a silly whine. He looked up through the hole in the fence. There on the opposite side of the yard, way up high, was Lizard Tongue, hanging over the top of the fence.

Benji almost choked on his tongue. He dashed away from the hole and peered around the corner by the back gate. That crazy dog was perched atop a tall stack of wobbling wooden shipping crates. How in the world did he get up there?

The shaggy mutt snorted and wagged his funny tail. *Hey, man. Just thought I'd drop by.*

Benji gawked at him.

Suddenly the stack of crates began to sway. Too much top-heavy tail-wagging. Lizard Tongue took a step backward and that was a bad move. The crates swayed in the other direction. Then one of them slipped, and that was it. The dog looked like a high-wire act trying to find his balance. A second later the stack came tumbling down with a loud crash.

"Who's there?!" Hatchett yelled from inside the yard.

Benji raced back to the hole in the fence and took a quick peek through. Sure enough, Hatchett was marching toward the back gate. Benji turned and raced off through the woods.

Lizard Tongue's head popped up from behind a box, apparently none the worse for wear. *Where'd everybody go?*

Just then Hatchett burst though the gate, saw Lizard Tongue and the mess, and screeched, "Get away from there, you filthy mongrel!"

The dog spun on his heels and ran after Benji.

10

The crickets were singing loudly that night as Benji waited for Mr. Finch's lights to go out. Apparently Mr. Finch liked to stay up late. Somewhere nearby an owl was hooting, and Benji could hear frogs down by the stream. A bright moon, almost full, made it seem nearly daylight when the last light in the house finally clicked off. Benji eased up to the porch and, sure enough, the bowl was full once again, this time with something much better than cereal. Quietly, he began his dinner.

The owl hooted again, causing Benji to peer out into the darkness enveloping the nearby forest. Somehow, instinctively, he knew that a big barn owl could weigh almost as much as he did, and that did not make him feel comfortable. Suddenly there was another sound, a creaking of some sort. Benji whipped around, gazing at the far end of the porch.

Nothing . . . until he looked up. There, easing out from between two of Mr. Finch's potted plants, high atop an old antique icebox that Mr. Finch had converted to a plant stand was Lizard Tongue!

Lizard Tongue!

Benji gaped at him. What was he doing here? How did he get up there? Had he followed Benji? This dog was rapidly becoming a pest. But it was amazing the way he just kept showing up everywhere.

Warf! Lizard Tongue whispered, tail wagging excitedly. *Can I share?*

Benji glanced back at the window, then door. Had Mr. Finch heard?

Apparently not. He snorted a frustrated snort. Very frustrated.

Lizard Tongue hopped down from the top of the icebox to a table full of smaller potted plants. Not a good idea. The minute his feet hit the table, his shoulder hit a small clay pot and sent it tumbling. It fell to the floor with a thud, shattering into tiny pieces.

Benji gawked at him, stunned. Lizard Tongue merely glanced at the shattered pot and seemed to brush it off. *Come on, it's just a pot.* And he leaped from the table to the floor.

It really wasn't that dark, so he should've seen the trowel laying across the bulb planter on the floor. Should have, but obviously didn't, because his right front foot slammed down onto the blade of the trowel, launching it into the air. Way into the air! The missile slammed against the front window.

Kerwham!

Then it dropped onto an antique metal milk crate.

Clangaram!

And finally onto the floor.

Kerthunk!

A light went on inside the house and Benji looked up at the window. Mr. Finch crossed in front of it, headed straight for the front door. Benji whipped his head around to glance back at Lizard Tongue.

What a ditz! He was just standing there with his snout in the bowl, chowing down. Benji turned and jumped off the porch, racing out into the night, still hungry.

Another lamp came on, bathing the porch in light. Lizard Tongue looked up to see Mr. Finch approaching the door, tying his bathrobe around him. The mutt grabbed a final mouthful of food from the bowl and dashed off the porch just as Mr. Finch stormed through the screen door.

"Hah! Caught you at last!" he said as he burst onto the porch. But the porch was now empty. No dog was to be seen anywhere. And not much had been eaten from the bowl. "Hmmm," he said, almost to himself. "Not very hungry tonight." Then he saw the shattered pot on the floor of the porch.

"I'll expect you to replace the flowerpot!" he hollered out toward the woods.

Around the corner, Lizard Tongue had finished his mouthful and was lying in the grass, waiting for Mr. Finch to go back inside. Benji had stopped at the edge of the forest and was peering back over his shoulder. He watched Mr. Finch retreat into the house. The old man seemed nice enough. A little blustery, but he did, after all, put food out. Getting too close, however, could result in all sorts of bad things happening, and Benji had work to do. It was just hard being all alone.

He turned away and loped off into the woods. The owl hooted again and it seemed closer, eliminating any thought Benji might have had about spending the night in the forest.

The old house, with all its drafts and creaking sounds, was better than being eaten by an owl. If only Benji could get some sleep. But sleep wouldn't come. The loneliness was giving way to fear, not for himself, but for his mom. She was so sick. There had to be a way to get her out of that backyard. There just had to be.

11

It was early. Roosters were still crowing off in the distance somewhere, but Benji was already peering through the hole in Hatchett's fence. He could see Daisy, lying on her side looking sick. The backyard was empty.

He trotted around to the back gate. A knotted rope hung from a hole in the top of the gate. On the other side, the rope was attached to the gate latch. Benji stood on his hind legs with his front paws on the gate, but the knot in the rope was out of reach. He tried jumping and almost caught it in his teeth a couple of times, but he just couldn't get it. He was so close.

He walked away and turned back to study the gate. There had to be a way. He lay down, dropping his chin onto a blanket of fallen leaves, staring at the knot in the rope. The boxes and crates that had tumbled down with Lizard Tongue were still lying about.

Boxes and crates!

That's it!

He pulled himself up, selected one of the smaller boxes, locked his teeth around an edge, and dragged the box over to the gate, positioning it just below the rope. It was just high enough to allow Benji to reach the knot on the end of the rope. He pulled down on it with all his weight. The latch popped and the gate swung open.

Kerthump!

The gate hit the box Benji was standing on and would open no further.

He snorted at the box, dropped to the ground, and dragged it out of the way. His heart pounded as he turned back to the gate, now standing ajar.

He nudged it further open with his nose, then peered inside at the backyard. It was still empty except for wailing puppies in the cages and barking dogs.

Daisy wasn't barking.

She was on her side looking very ill, but she sensed Benji's presence and turned her head toward the gate. Benji could feel the happiness in her eyes when she saw him standing there.

He walked to her cage and stood on his hind legs. They were almost nose-to-nose. Benji's heart sank seeing his mom in such bad condition. Her eyes were glazed over and runny, and her face was caked with dried mucus. He glanced at the latch on the cage door and began trying to nudge it upward with his nose. It was old and rusty and difficult to move, but he knew he could do it.

Just then, the back door swung open. It was Colby. He spotted Benji immediately and didn't know exactly what to make of his presence. He glanced over his shoulder, concerned that Hatchett might see. Colby eased the screen door shut and watched.

Benji finally had gotten his nose under the bolt of the latch, just enough to lift it. Suddenly he heard a loud, way-too-familiar bark. He whipped around, and there was Lizard Tongue hanging over the top of the fence on the far side of the back yard.

Warf!

Who is that? Colby wondered.

Lizard Tongue was happy to see Benji.

The reverse was not true. Benji flicked a glance over his shoulder at the back door of the house. Had anyone heard? He saw Colby standing just inside the door and his heart leaped into his throat. When he looked back at Lizard Tongue, the stupid dog was struggling across the top of the fence, dangling by his belly, trying to jump down onto the tops of several garbage cans right below him. Unbelievable! Benji could see it coming before it happened. Lizard Tongue lost his grip on the fence, slipped off, and crashed headlong into the garbage cans below him.

Kerwham-bang-crash!

Like a row of dominoes falling, half a dozen old metal garbage cans came smashing to the ground, spilling their contents all over the yard!

"What's going on out there?" Hatchett's voice echoed out of the house.

Benji's feet hit the ground, and he was gone. Just as Hatchett burst through the screen door onto the porch, Benji was out the gate.

Lizard Tongue was crawling out of the mess, completely un-harmed, a piece of dried lettuce hanging onto his face.

"You again! You the one been getting to my females, you scum of a mongrel?"

Lizard Tongue gave him a friendly woof and trotted obliviously right over to the bottom step of the porch.

"Ain't you the dumb one," said Hatchett. "Come 'ere, let me get my hands around your straggly neck."

Hatchett eased down onto the first step off the porch. Then another step.

Lizard Tongue's long-ago broken tail whipped the air like a fan. Suddenly, there was a different bark. Loud and anxious.

Everybody looked to the gate where Benji was barking, barking, barking! Frantically! *Come on. Get outta there!*

Lizard Tongue looked back at Hatchett. *Is there a problem here?*

Hatchett was suddenly frozen in place, his old loathing for Benji overruling his new loathing for Lizard Tongue. Behind him, Colby took a step forward, worried about what would happen. Hatchett went for Benji. He was barely off the porch when Colby leaped into the air, landing on Hatchett's back, arms wrapped around his neck.

"No!" Colby screeched. "You leave him alone."

Benji barked one last time at Lizard Tongue, then whirled around and raced out of the backyard. Lizard Tongue looked up at Hatchett, who was slinging Colby to the ground, and decided he better be on his way. He made a beeline for the gate.

Colby hit the ground with a thud that knocked the breath out of him. Hatchett stood over him seething, furious, on the edge. But after a long moment, all he said was, "Feed the dogs." Then he turned and stalked into the house.

"Now!" he added as the screen door slammed behind him.

Colby pulled himself off the ground and walked over to the open gate, wondering exactly how Benji had managed to get in. He saw the box, glanced at the height of the latch rope, and smiled to himself. Then he had an idea. He glanced over his shoulder to make sure Hatchett wasn't watching, then picked up a small sliver of wood off the ground and jammed it in behind the mechanism of the gate latch, holding it open so it couldn't latch. He eased the gate closed and walked over to Daisy's cage, opened the door, and scratched her warmly on her head.

"Don't worry, girl," he said. "He'll be back."

12

Benji was as frustrated as a dog could be. He was lying under the lean-to in the woods, trying to ignore the antics of Lizard Tongue prancing around just outside, happy as could be, completely oblivious to Benji's frustration.

Warf! Come on, let's play!

Benji snorted a tiny sigh and turned away. He had been so close to getting Daisy's cage door open when this troublemaker crashed in and blew the whole thing.

Lizard Tongue barked again, and sat down in the leaves. He, too, was frustrated because he didn't understand why he couldn't get Benji to play, to romp and have a good time. *Life is for fun, right?* He turned a couple of circles and then crawled under the lean-to, nuzzling up close to Benji.

Benji scooted away.

Lizard Tongue blinked and pondered, then crawled sideways right next to him again.

Benji was out of room, so he simply turned his head away. He wanted to be left alone.

Lizard Tongue's chin dropped onto the leaves that covered the ground under the lean-to. He looked quite pitiful, probably by design, but won no attention from Benji. Finally, he pulled himself out onto the path, and with a last cheerless look at Benji, he turned and trotted off down the path. Before he was out of sight, he spotted a squirrel and was off after it.

Benji sighed as his worries flooded back. He was afraid for his mom.

On the other side of the woods, the dogcatchers had turned up at Mr. Finch's house. As they approached the porch, Mr. Finch was ignoring them, digging away at one of his potted plants. Livingston knocked on one of the porch columns and cleared his throat. Finally Mr. Finch looked up.

"Yes. Something I can do for you?"

Livingston stood tall, shoulders back, acting as important as he could.

"I believe there is, uhhh . . ."—he checked a note in a small notebook—"Mr. Zachariah Finch?"

"One and the same."

"We understand you've had a stray dog coming around on occasion."

Finch turned from his planting table, pot and trowel in hand, and walked to the pair.

"Now how would you be understanding something like that?"

Sheldon took a step forward. "That would be none of

your business, now would it?" He got nasty looks from both Livingston and Finch, and took a quick step backward. "Or maybe, it would be. I don't know, what do you think, Livingston?"

Livingston sighed and flipped a page in his notepad, showing it to Finch.

"One Dudley Morrison. I believe he delivers your groceries. Says you've been buying dog food lately, but you don't seem to have a dog."

Sheldon stepped up again. "And I believe there's some of that dog food right over there in that—"

He turned to look at the bowl on the porch and gagged on his words. Lizard Tongue was standing there, less than four feet away, munching away on the food in the bowl.

"It's him!" He grabbed Livingston by the arm. "It's Lizard Tongue!"

Livingston turned to look. Finch stretched to peer between them. Surprised, he smiled, then quickly wiped the grin from his face before the dogcatchers could turn back.

"Is this your dog?" said Livingston as sternly as he could.

"Because if it is," blurted Sheldon, "you're in big trouble. He's been running loose all over the *counnghh!*"

Sheldon was stopped cold by an elbow in the ribs from Livingston.

"Sorry about my associate. He's an idiot. But I do need to know if this is your dog."

Finch stretched for another look.

"I don't see a dog. Do you see a dog?"

Neither dogcatcher wanted to turn around, knowing full well what was waiting for them.

And they were right. No dog. Nothing but the food bowl.

"I put that food out there for the otters," said Finch, strolling back to his worktable to deposit the trowel and pot he still held in his hands. Livingston looked at him quizzically.

"The otters?"

"Yes," said Finch. "Good to have around. They keep the bears away."

"We don't have any bears in the these parts."

Sheldon nodded.

"There, you see," said Finch with a smile. "It's the otters."

He strolled toward the screen door.

"Now if you gentlemen will excuse me, I have a soufflé in the oven." And he disappeared into the house.

"Wait," said Livingston. "Mr. Finch, I have a few more questions!"

No response.

Livingston turned away from the door, not at all sure how he had lost control.

"He is the devil, you know," said Sheldon.

"Mr. Finch?"

"That dog! He's messin' with our minds!"

"Did you know that about otters?" Livingston stepped off the porch, headed toward their van.

"I don't care about otters," said Sheldon, falling in behind

Livingston. "I wanna know what happened to that mutt."

"I think it's interesting," Livingston continued. "I mean, if a little bitty otter can intimidate a great big bear . . ."

Sheldon interrupted, "It's no different than a little bitty dog intimidating two great big men."

Livingston stopped suddenly, raising a hand for Sheldon to do the same.

"I feel like we're being followed."

Sheldon grimaced, and began to quiver.

"Lizard Tongue?"

A tiny nod from Livingston accompanied a slow turn. Sure enough, not ten feet behind them, tail a-wagging, was Lizard Tongue.

Wa-ar-arff!

Sheldon wanted to screech. Livingston grabbed his arm.

"Be calm. We can do this. We just have to be calm. Can't chase him. We have to become his buddies. His friends."

Sheldon's breath was erratic and he was trembling. "I–I–I can't do that. This is Lizard Tongue you're talking about. Your butt doesn't still hurt because of Lizard Tongue! I still have mud up my nose because of Lizard Tongue!"

"Just follow my lead and this will be a snap." Livingston put a smile on his face and addressed the goofy mutt before them. "Hi there, Lizard Tongue. How're you doing today? Isn't this a great day? And we're your buds, you know? Yeah. What say we go for a walk. C'mon."

He turned away and strode toward the woods, dragging

Colby on his way to visit Benji and his siblings.

Colby takes care of Daisy and her pups at the abandoned house.

Benji!

Benji and Lizard Tongue on a mission . . .

. . . and at Animal Control
Headquarters.

Colby checks up on Merlin and the fort.

Hatchett confronts Colby.

Lizard Tongue sneaks around Mr. Finch's house.

Mr. Finch looks for the mystery dog.

The dogcatchers search for Lizard Tongue.

Lizard Tongue plays hide-and-seek with Animal Control.

Lizard Tongue is afraid to cross the log.

Lizard Tongue and Benji escape the hard way!

Sick Daisy in the old abandoned house.

Colby and Daisy make a tough decision.

Sheldon along. After a moment, Lizard Tongue fell in behind them, keeping his distance, but following nonetheless.

"Right on, huh, Sheldon? A friendly walk in the woods."

Sheldon glanced over his shoulder and tried to grin at Lizard Tongue. Not very successfully. "Yeah. A friendly walk in the woods." He still wasn't sure exactly what Livingston had in mind until he saw him unsnap the strap on the tranquilizer gun. Livingston began to sing a song of his own making.

"Just a friendly walk in the woo-oo-oods with the tranquilizer gu-uh-uh-un."

Then he whispered to Sheldon, "We need to get him close, so be calm. Don't chase him."

"Gotcha."

And they disappeared into the woods whistling a happy tune.

13

Benji found the hole in the fence and peered through into the backyard. A shiver skittered down his back. Hatchett stood fewer than twenty feet away, sloshing water into a dog bowl with a hose. He stalked to Daisy's cage and dropped the bowl right by her face, splashing water into her eyes. She didn't move and didn't even seem to notice.

Benji watched him disappear into the house, then turned away from the hole and eased to the corner of the fence, peering around at the gate. He stepped out toward the gate when a loud familiar warff stopped him in his tracks. He spun toward the sound, and sure enough, there was Lizard Tongue, racing right at him from across a small pasture. Sheldon and Livingston were not far behind, climbing over a rail fence.

"I told you not to chase him!" screamed Livingston.

Lizard Tongue raced right by Benji's nose and slid to a stop not far away.

Warf!

Benji glanced at the approaching dogcatchers, not thirty feet away.

- *War-ar-arff!*

Then Lizard Tongue was gone. Off toward the woods.

With a last look at the knotted rope dangling from the gate latch, Benji snorted and leaped out after Lizard Tongue. In a flash they had both disappeared into the forest. As Lizard Tongue rounded a tree and raced off down a well-worn path, Benji passed him and took the lead. The dog-catchers were actually running a good race, losing a bit of ground, but hanging in not too far back, leaping logs, dodging trees. Men on a mission.

Benji knew exactly where he was going. Not far ahead was a wide stream. And only one way across. A log, lying across the stream. Benji could cross it. Lizard Tongue could cross it. But the two men behind them? Not a chance. Especially the big dumpy one.

Benji hit the log on the run and raced across, turning on the far side. Lizard Tongue skidded to a stop, eyes nervously fixed on the log. And the water. Benji barked, and barked again. *Come on, stupid.*

But Lizard Tongue was clearly afraid. He glanced behind him. The dogcatchers had not yet emerged from the trees. He tested the log with one foot, then took it back. Then tried again. Benji was barking frantically. *What is the matter with that dog?!*

The dogcatchers burst out of the woods. Livingston had

the tranquilizer gun at the ready. They spotted the two dogs. On the far side of the stream, Benji was barking. On the near side, Lizard Tongue was stepping on the log, then off again. Then on again. Livingston rounded the bend in the path and raced down the hill toward the stream, raising the tranquilizer gun as he came. Lizard Tongue spun to face them, then turned and raced away from the log.

The pistol was up! The trigger pulled.

Kerfwoot!

The dart embedded itself into the trunk of a tree just as Lizard Tongue disappeared behind it. A near miss.

Sheldon raced past Livingston. "Come on," he grumbled, disgusted with Livingston's aim. Then he, too, disappeared behind the tree.

Livingston looked across the stream at Benji, and Benji tensed, wondering what the tall man might do next. With a frustrated sigh, Livingston dashed off after Sheldon.

Benji watched them race off along the stream and vanish into the forest. Then he snorted.

Not far away, Lizard Tongue burst into a green meadow and before he realized where he was, he had dashed around a stand of bushes and was screeching to a stop at the edge of the river bluff! That same river way down there! He considered jumping, but only for a moment, then he turned and started back toward the meadow as Sheldon and Livingston raced around the stand of bushes. Lizard Tongue was trapped.

"Spread out. Go slow," said Livingston. They began to creep toward Lizard Tongue.

The scruffy mutt took a step backward. His happy-go-lucky demeanor had vanished.

The two men in blue were spreading out and advancing. Livingston's tranquilizer gun was up and ready to fire. Sheldon was crouching, ready to pounce, easing toward the dog.

Lizard Tongue took another step backward and his foot slipped over the edge. He caught himself and glanced behind him and down, at the swirling river below. Panic was setting in. He glanced at Livingston.

The gun was up. Livingston was taking aim. Lizard Tongue glanced back. There was nowhere to go. Livingston's finger tightened on the trigger—when, out of nowhere, came a bark.

A loud bark. Somewhere behind the dogcatchers. Livingston whirled around.

Benji was standing in the meadow, staring straight at Livingston. He leaped out of the tall grass and seemed to lope straight for the dogcatcher with the gun. Before Livingston could react, Benji ran right between his legs.

Benji was racing straight at Lizard Tongue, digging at the ground, pulling with every muscle, closer and closer. Sheldon and Livingston were turning, mouths agape, starting after him, but they were too late.

Benji plowed into Lizard Tongue at full speed, right into his chest, driving them both off into the wild blue yonder. The two dogs, paws thrashing the air, howls echoing through the woods, sailed down from the bluff arching toward the river.

Ker-splash!

Ker-splash!

Benji and Lizard Tongue hit the water and begin swimming for their lives toward the far bank. High above, standing on the bluff, Livingston and Sheldon just stared incredulously at the spectacle. Livingston's arms were flailing the air.

"How can this happen?!" he screeched. "How, how, how?!"

The two sopping pups dragged themselves out of the river on the far bank and each had a good shake. Lizard Tongue warfed and snorted. *That was fun!*

Benji gawked at him, amused, then turned and trotted off up the bank.

Hey wait.

Lizard Tongue followed. They were bound together now. After all, Benji had saved his life.

14

It was broad daylight when Benji peered around the corner of Mr. Finch's house, scanning the porch and the grounds. He had not been here during the day since the first time. It had been too risky. But there was no movement in sight. He glanced behind him then trotted off toward the porch. Lizard Tongue appeared at the corner and promptly followed.

The food bowl was full. Waiting. But Benji didn't eat. He nudged it in Lizard Tongue's direction with his nose.

Lizard Tongue stopped and gawked at him. *What's the catch?*

Benji nudged it again.

Lizard Tongue cocked his head. But didn't move.

One more nudge. And a soft woof. *Come on.*

Okay, if you insist. Lizard Tongue licked his chops and dove in.

Benji eased backward away from Lizard Tongue, toward the screen door leading into Finch's house. He dug at it softly

with his foot, prying it open, and he slipped right inside.
Lizard Tongue was crunching away, oblivious.

"Do I know you?"

It was Finch's voice, from inside.

"Wait."

Benji reappeared, slipping through the door and down the
edge of the porch behind Lizard Tongue, then off behind the
house.

Lizard Tongue crunched away at the fine nuggets in the
bowl until Finch appeared at the door.

"Well, well, well."

Lizard Tongue spun around, freaked. He looked around
for Benji, but he was nowhere to be seen.

"I think you've been abandoned," said Finch. He eased
out onto the porch and held out a friendly hand to Lizard
Tongue.

Lizard Tongue took a nervous step backward.

"It's okay. I'm not going to hurt you." Finch pulled away
from him.

"Go ahead, eat."

He nudged the bowl toward Lizard Tongue with his foot.

"Go on. Eat your fill. I'll just sit over here and rest my
bones. Talk to the weeds." Finch eased over to an old antique
milk crate and sat down on it, right at the edge of the porch,
looking off toward the woods.

"It's a cold, cruel world out there, you know. Hard to get
along, just on your own. Nobody to talk to." He glanced at

Lizard Tongue. "Don'tcha think?"

Lizard Tongue allowed the slightest wag of his crooked tail. He wanted to go to him, but didn't. Too nervous.

"What happened to that tail? Looks like you were waggin' when you should've been runnin'." Finch gazed off toward the woods again. "If I don't pay you no mind, I'll betcha you'll wiggle yourself right over here in a minute."

Lizard Tongue wanted to. He pranced, tongue dangling, tail wagging. Finch glanced slyly at him.

"That, Mr. Shaggy Dog, is the longest tongue I've ever seen."

Lizard Tongue took a step closer and Finch stretched out a hand and gave him a scratch on the head. Then, he pulled away, gazing off toward the front yard.

"Yeah, I can see you've been out there on those streets a while. All you need is a bit of good ole' fashioned TLC, and I can do that," he said, peering over his bifocals. "So long as you don't tell anybody," he chuckled.

Lizard Tongue took a step closer, then another, but Finch pretended to ignore him. Finally, with a wag of his crooked tail, Lizard Tongue took the last step and nuzzled his nose under the old man's hand. Finch smiled and picked him up into his lap, and Lizard Tongue licked him in the face.

"Who's your friend out there?"

Benji was standing out near the edge of the woods watching the developments on the porch. There was a sadness in his eyes. Lizard Tongue was getting a scratch, then a hug. And he was licking Finch in the face. Benji missed that, missed that a lot. But there was work to do. And now he might just be able to get to it.

He turned and vanished into the woods.

15

A spoon dipped into creamy white liquid and rose to a mouth. Hatchett's mouth.

"Soup's ice-cold," he grumbled, his words as cold as the soup.

"It's supposed to be cold," said Claire. "It's cold potato soup."

"I like my soup hot." He pushed it aside.

"It's French," said Colby. He was sitting opposite Hatchett, who had his back to the open double doors into the back-yard. "It's called vichyssoise."

Hatchett slammed the table.

"I don't care what it's called! I like my soup hot! It ain't soup if it's cold. It's something else."

Colby glanced at his mom, and sighed. Then, a movement caught his eye, over Hatchett's shoulder, out in the backyard. The gate was moving. Then a nose appeared and nudged through.

It was Benji.

Colby almost lost his mouthful of soup. He tried desperately to look nonchalant, but inside he was smiling. The chip of wood he had left in the gate latch had worked.

Benji glanced toward the house, then eased over to Daisy's cage. He stood on his hind legs, front feet on the cage, and woofed softly at his mom.

Colby tried to blink it away, not wanting to attract attention. He gathered another spoonful of soup, tossed a nervous glance at Hatchett, and stole another look outside.

Benji was lifting the latch with his nose! Actually lifting it, and trying to sling it over, out of the lock. It was all Colby could do to not race out and help.

It was a struggle for Benji. Holding the latch up while trying to move it out of the lock wasn't easy, especially with just a nose. But finally with one smart slinging motion, it worked.

Click.

The latch was open. Daisy rolled over onto her belly and looked up at her son.

Benji woofed. Softly. Then he scratched at the door to the cage. It swung open.

Inside the house, Hatchett suddenly slammed the table.

Benji spun toward the screen door.

"Macaroni's cold too," Hatchett bellowed.

Benji dropped down to the ground and backed off a step. He woofed at his mom. *Come on. You can do it.*

"It's cold pasta salad," said Claire. "This is a light summer dinner."

Hatchett stood up from the table, plate in hand.

"At the end of the day, when I've been working since dawn, I want a good hot meal! With some meat! Not some pansy Frenchy stuff. Is that clear?!"

Benji reacted to the noise and woofed again at Daisy, urging her on.

She pulled herself toward the cage door.

Hatchett strode toward the kitchen counter and Colby leaped out of his chair, grabbing him just in time to keep him from turning toward the backyard.

"It'll be okay," he said, as nicely as he could while sneaking a glance out the window. "Just sit down and I'll make you a big bowl of hot bean soup. I can do that great!" He shoved Hatchett toward his chair and pushed him into it. Hatchett was astonished. So was Claire.

"Colby . . . ?"

"It's fine, Mom. You two just sit and enjoy each other. That's it. Just enjoy each other. This won't take a minute."

Hatchett was wondering what the devil had come over his kid. He was acting way out of character. Could he be coming to his senses?

Colby hurried off to the pantry.

Daisy dropped from the cage to the ground. Her wobbly legs almost gave way, but she managed to stand, just barely. She tried to reach out and lick Benji's face, but Benji pulled away, anxious to get her out of the backyard. He glanced at the house, then woofed softly, and turned toward the gate.

Daisy took a step toward the gate, and her head dropped in pain. She stood for a long moment, then took another step. Benji darted and danced and urged, moving ever closer to the gate. Then he woofed again.

At the kitchen table, Hatchett was standing again, and, once more, Colby raced over and pushed him down in his chair. "It'll just be a minute," he said.

"Leave me be, boy, I'm just getting a beer."

"Mom will get that for you," he said, turning to Claire.

"Wrong! I'm not getting him a beer."

"Mom!" Colby gave her a look that said *please!* "We goofed up his dinner. Now, we gotta make it up to him." Another look. *Go! Please!*

Outside, Benji paced nervously at the gate as Daisy took one slow, painful step after another, plodding toward the way out, until finally she was there. Benji turned and disappeared through the gate, but Daisy just stared at the opening, not at all sure she could take another step.

Hatchett sat at the table, arms folded, suddenly quite full of himself. This is the way it's supposed to be. He stood up and turned toward the backyard. Colby's spoon hit the floor and the noise turned Hatchett back. Once again, Colby raced over and tried to forcibly sit Hatchett back in his chair.

"I'm just gonna grab my paper out on the porch," Hatchett said.

Colby used all his strength to shove him down in the chair.

"I told you, we're here to take care of you! Mom will get your paper."

He turned to Claire. "Won't you, Mom?" The words were accompanied by another pleading look. Claire was mystified at what in the world was going on with her son, but she pulled herself out of her chair and walked toward the back porch.

As she opened the screen door, she knew immediately what Colby's strange behavior was all about. Daisy's cage was wide open. The fence gate was wide open. And Daisy was nowhere in sight. Claire's eyes dropped shut, and she shuddered at what would soon hit the fan.

She picked up the newspaper off Hatchett's chair, turned, and retreated inside.

16

The headlights pierced the dark night, squealing around the corner, headed for the old abandoned house. The green pickup screeched to a stop at the rusty old front gate and Hatchett climbed out, flashlight in hand.

"Come on!"

Colby didn't move from the passenger seat.

"I'm telling you, I had nothing to do with it! I have no idea where she is!" The truth was he was pretty sure they were in the house, and he didn't want Hatchett to find them.

Hatchett was already stomping toward the front door. He turned. "Get your butt outta that truck now! We're gonna find out!"

Colby dragged himself out of the truck and plodded toward Hatchett.

"Why would she be here?"

Hatchett grabbed Colby by the arm and dragged him

along to the front door. "Because this is where you put her last time!"

"I didn't put her here last time," Colby pleaded, pulling away from Hatchett's grasp. "And if I did, why would I be so stupid to bring her here again?"

Hatchett spun around and sizzled right into his face. "Because you think I'm stupid, that's why! But we'll find out who's stupid, won't we?!" And he whirled and stomped off toward the front door, dragging Colby behind him.

Hatchett searched every room in the house, his flashlight piercing the darkness under beds, tables, in closets and dusty, cobwebbed corners. Colby could barely watch as Hatchett stomped into each new room, afraid of what he might find. But there was no Benji. And no Daisy.

Hatchett burst angrily back onto the front porch, his flashlight splashing all across the front yard.

Still nothing.

Finally, he stomped off toward the truck. Colby stepped out of the front door and eased it closed, then quickly changed his mind, and left it slightly ajar. He smiled and headed for the rusty green pickup.

The truck squealed off down the street, and once again the neighborhood was still and quiet . . . until Benji's face emerged from behind a large bush in the front yard. He watched the pickup truck disappear into the darkness, then turned to the bush and woofed softly. Moments later, Daisy limped out from under the bush and followed Benji into the old abandoned house.

The phone was ringing early the next morning at the animal shelter in Gulfport. Miriam, the shelter director, had not even had her coffee when she snatched the phone off the hook.

"South County Animal Care and Control."

She listened for a long moment, brow furrowing. Then a slight and sly smile sneaked across her face. She grabbed a pen and began to write.

"Oh, I know very well who you are, Mr. Hatchett. You're rather well documented around here."

She pushed away from the desk and strolled across the room toward a tall file cabinet, phone in hand.

"Is that a fact? And you're asking us for help?"

She pulled opened a drawer and dug around for a particular file.

"I see. I'm amazed." Withdrawing a tattered file folder, she returned to her desk.

"No, no. Rest assured, we'll be on the lookout for your dog. And if we find her, we'll definitely give you a call."

She hung up the phone.

"Or not."

She reached for the walkie-talkie on her desk and depressed the "talk" button. "Base to unit one. Unit one, come in."

Sheldon and Livingston were in their van wandering the streets of town searching for their catch of the day. Sheldon reached for the walkie-talkie on the dash but Livingston snatched it away. "This is unit one, over."

He listened as Miriam said, "I just received a very interesting phone call. . . ."

17

The alley behind Mr. Paul's market was hot that morning, and smells of all kinds drifted from the lineup of rusty old, battered trash cans.

Benji watched as Mr. Paul backed out of the door with an apron full of early garbage. He trudged to the nearest can, slid the lid to one side, and emptied his apron's contents onto yesterday's spoils. A big fat roasted turkey leg landed right on top. Mr. Paul did not notice Benji watching him. He turned and retreated back into the market.

Less than half an hour later, Benji was back at the old abandoned house with the turkey leg. He dropped it in front of Daisy and nudged it toward her mouth. She was lying on her side, breathing heavily, and only blinked at the prospect of food. She didn't budge. Benji nudged the turkey leg closer, closer, but Daisy wouldn't eat. He licked her face and paced away.

Daisy was sick. Really sick. And Benji didn't know what to do. He paced frustrating circles around the room, finally lying down next to his mom, chin on the floor, eyes flitting from her to the turkey leg to the window, through which the only light in the room streamed.

Wait a minute! What's that?

An ugly orange van.

Benji strolled across the room and put his feet up on the windowsill for a better look. It was those silly dogcatchers in the blue shirts, creeping by, just outside the window.

Suddenly he had an idea.

The van pulled away down the street. Sheldon was ranting and waving his arms. "Well, I think you're wrong! That old house would be a good hideout. Nobody lives there."

"How would she get in?" questioned Livingston. "Besides, dogs are going where people are, where they can get food. They don't have sense enough to hide out."

"Don't tell me they don't have sense. Lizard Tongue has plenty of sense." Sheldon pointed at himself with pride. "So far, he's managed to outwit me!"

Livingston gave him a look. *That certainly proves nothing.*

"I just can't believe that jerk had the gall to call and ask us for help," said Livingston. "We who'd love nothing better than to nail him good! This could be our big chance if we could just get our hands on that dog."

Sheldon could see the size of this opportunity. This could be their big chance.

"Yeah, if we can just get our hands on that dog, we'll . . . we'll . . ."

He turned to Livingston with a blank look on his face.

"We'll do what?"

Livingston shook his head and sighed.

"We'll give her a complete medical work up for starters. Examine her from top to bottom, so to speak. Check her for signs of cruelty, for overbreeding. Whatever is wrong with her, we can lay on Hatchett. We'll have evidence to take him to court."

He grinned at Sheldon, who was suddenly gasping at something through the front windshield.

"Stop the car!"

Livingston jammed the brake pedal. Wheels locked, tires squealed, and the van screeched to a long, excruciating stop, less than a yard away from Benji. He was sitting calmly right in the middle of the street. He neither moved nor blinked.

"It's the Tongue's buddy," gasped Sheldon.

"Almost not," replied Livingston.

"Let's get him!"

Sheldon was halfway out the door when Livingston grabbed his arm.

"Hold it, we have to focus on the priority."

"Right."

Sheldon blinked.

"Which is?"

"The missing dog!" pressed Livingston. "The one that'll nail Hatchett."

"Exactly." Sheldon looked at Benji. "But what about this one?"

Benji hadn't moved a muscle. Still in the middle of the street, gazing straight at them.

"I guarantee the minute you make a move toward him, he's gone. And we don't have time to chase him halfway to Chicago."

"C'mon. He'd never get that far. Maybe Hattiesburg."

That brought another impatient sigh from Livingston. "Get him outta the street and let's go."

Sheldon climbed out of the van and lumbered straight toward Benji. Benji waited until the very last moment to bound off onto the sidewalk and down the street, fully expecting Sheldon to follow him. They always chase. *That's what they do!* But when he turned back, Sheldon was climbing back into the van, which then drove off down the street, right past him.

These people didn't understand.

This was frustrating.

Something had to be done.

18

Ozzie pulled on the last slurp of a fast-food milkshake. He dusted a few crumbs off his deputy uniform and set the empty cup on Miriam's desk.

"All the same, I don't see how you deal with it everyday. It's a depressing job."

He and Miriam had been friends for a long time, but Ozzie had never understood how anyone could face putting animals to sleep on a daily basis.

Miriam wiped a bit of mustard from her lip. "And yours, isn't?"

"My job is about helping people."

That drew a look from across the desk.

"*Most* of the time," Ozzie added.

"Mine's about helping people too," she said, tossing down the last bite of her sandwich. "By helping animals."

"Yeah, but look at how many you have to, you know."

"Not nearly as many as when I started here, and I can feel good about that."

She wadded her trash into a ball and tossed it into file thirteen.

"Anyway, finish up and get outta here. I've got work to do."

Ozzie dumped his trash and headed for the door.

As he reached for the knob, Miriam stopped him.

"Ozzie, wait a minute. I've got a situation here, and wondered if maybe—"

"Uh-oh."

Miriam forced a sweet smile. "It's just a little favor."

The dogcatchers' orange van rounded a corner onto Magnolia Street, and eased to a stop.

"We've been down this street before," said Sheldon.

"I don't think so," replied Livingston.

"I know so."

"How do you know so?"

"Because," said Sheldon, "there's that dog again."

Livingston stretched to see out Sheldon's window. Sure enough, Benji was sitting on the sidewalk, gazing up at Sheldon. He woofed. A loud one.

"What's with him? It's like he wants us to nab him," said Sheldon.

"I don't know. It's weird. Maybe he's bored."

"Maybe he wants us to follow him," said Sheldon. Then, a thought struck him. "Maybe he knows where the black dog is."

"Oh, right! Like in the Lassie movies, where the dog was

smarter than the people."

"Exactly," said Sheldon. "I mean, it's possible."

Livingston sighed in exasperation, and shifted into gear. "In your case it's *probable*!"

The van drove off down the street.

Benji snorted. This was not the way it was supposed to work.

Back at the animal shelter, Ozzie was propped against the door to Miriam's office, picking his teeth with a toothpick. "Gee, I don't know. We really need some kind of probable cause. Something that'll get us in the door."

"Sheldon and Livingston have seen the backyard," Miriam countered. "They're pretty sure the dog cages don't conform to the law."

"Sheldon and Livingston? I wouldn't want to rest my case on those two."

"My point exactly. That's why I want you out there. To check it out for yourself. At the very least, make him nervous. Let him know he's being watched."

"How could he not know with the Bumble Twins snooping around?"

Miriam gave him a chiding look. "Ozzie. . . ."

Ozzie sighed. "Why don't we wait? If you find this black dog, and if she's been abused, then we'll have a good reason."

"Ozzie, this is not a nice guy. His dogs are being treated very poorly. It's clear he doesn't care about them except for the puppies he can sell. There's no telling what all is going on out there and—"

Ozzie raised both hands in defense.

"Okay, okay. Let me do some research. What's the guy's name?"

"Hatchett." She glanced at the file spread out on her desk. "Terrence Muncie Hatchett."

That rang a bell with Ozzie. Not a nice one.

"Lives out east? Just out of town?"

Miriam nodded.

Ozzie dug back through his memory, trying to put his finger on what was bothering him.

"What?"

"Not sure," Ozzie said. "Let me check it. I'll call you."

"Thanks, Oz."

She was grateful to have a friend like him. He was more than a friend, actually. This is why she didn't like asking him for favors. But she felt this one was necessary. Miriam watched him through the glass wall in her office as he nodded at the receptionist and left through the front door. She had always loved his honesty and compassion. He was a good man, she thought. Not too many of those around.

19

"**I** don't know why I let you drag me out here," said Livingston.

"Because this is the last place we saw that black dog," Sheldon retorted.

"Uhh, ohhh!" squawked Merlin.

The dogcatchers were peering through the tiny window of Colby's fort. Merlin paced nervously on his limb inside the fort.

"Empty," said Livingston. "Nada. Zero."

"Nada. Zero. Get rid of the bird," said Merlin.

"I'll bet the bird knows where she is."

They eased around to the front door to the fort.

"The dog knows. The bird knows," grumbled Livingston. "Who are you, Dr. Dolittle?"

They peered in through a hole in the door.

"I might be. They all laughed at him too, in the beginning."

Livingston turned away. "C'mon. Let's go."

He stopped with a jolt.

There, not ten feet away, sprawled in a thatch of leaves was Benji.

He woofed. *Hello again.*

"I'm telling you, Livingston, we should follow this dog. He's telling us something."

Livingston turned to Sheldon and screeched in his face.

"What exactly is he telling us?! What?"

"Well, he, he," Sheldon paused, then squared his shoulders and faced his partner. "You think I'm being stupid, don't you?"

"In a word, yes! Come on."

And Livingston stomped off down the path through the woods. Sheldon looked at Benji, took a deep breath, stood very tall, and spoke to him. Right to him as if he expected Benji to understand.

"Don't you give up. You hear me? No matter how hard it gets, no matter how long it takes. You can do this. You can rise above the simple folk who think animals are dumb, who think—"

"Sheldon!" screamed Livingston from somewhere out in the woods.

"Coming," he said, then turned back to Benji and gave him two thumbs-up. "Just remember. Keep the faith. You can do this."

Then, he disappeared into the woods.

Benji's chin dropped into the leaves. Communicating with

humans was difficult. They chased when it wasn't important, and did nothing when it was.

Meanwhile, Daisy was getting no help.

Then suddenly, an idea! And he was off, racing out into the woods.

The phone was ringing at the animal shelter.

It had been ringing all day! Or so it seemed to Miriam. She snatched it off the receiver.

"Hey, it's me," said Ozzie. "I was right. This guy Hatchett has a record."

"Animal abuse?" asked Miriam.

"People abuse. His wife and their kid. He was given a stiff warning and promised it would never happen again."

"We can't wait, Ozzie. We gotta dig this guy out. We don't want to say we had the chance to stop something and didn't."

"I'll pay him a friendly little visit."

"Thanks, Ozzie."

20

All was quiet outside the Finch house. Inside, a TV blared out an afternoon game show. Benji wasn't exactly sure how to go about this, so he trotted right up to the screen door and peered in. Finch was asleep on the couch, and Lizard Tongue was in his lap, also snoring loudly.

Benji woofed.

Nothing.

Again. Louder. Louder than the TV. And Lizard Tongue's eyes popped open. Did he hear something?

Benji issued a full bark.

Lizard Tongue turned to the door.

Hey, how've you been?

He crawled out of Finch's lap and trotted over to the door. Benji retreated to the grass, and waited.

Lizard Tongue nudged through the screen door and circled Benji a couple of times, sniffing and snorting. Then, quite suddenly, Benji turned and left.

Huh?

Several yards away, he paused, looked back, and barked. A big one. *Come on.*

Lizard Tongue didn't get it. He glanced back at the house. *I like it here.*

Benji trotted still farther away and barked again! *I need your help!*

Lizard Tongue took a long look at the warm cozy house, with food, and a caring human. *It's stupid to leave this.*

But Benji was insistent. He barked again, sternly. Then he turned and trotted off across the lawn, and didn't look back.

This was the dog who had saved his life. Twice. With one last long look at the house, Lizard Tongue reluctantly stepped off the porch and followed his friend. Benji broke into a run, and Lizard Tongue accelerated after him. *Who knows? Maybe whatever this is will be fun.*

21

Ozzie gathered himself for a task he didn't relish, then crawled out of the squad car and headed for Hatchett's front door. An old rattling convertible pulled into the driveway.

Ozzie sighed. Donnie Madison was the last person he wanted to see right now. The tall, lanky man leaped over the door of the convertible and galloped toward Ozzie, his garish Hawaiian shirt blowing in the breeze.

"What do you want?" Ozzie queried, not very politely.

"C'mon, Ozzie. Don't be silly. You know I scan the police radio. This is big! You gonna arrest him? Take him to jail?" Donnie dug into a pocket. "No, wait. Let me turn on the recorder."

Ozzie grabbed his hand and held it firmly.

"Do not turn on the recorder. Do not follow me up there. Do get into your car and drive away from here immediately." He grabbed Donnie's ear and lead him back to his car.

"Aw, come on, Ozzie. Give me a break. My listeners want to know."

Ozzie jerked open the car door and shoved Donnie into the driver's seat.

"Know this. If you're not outta here in ten seconds, you're going to be broadcasting from a jail cell."

"At least tell me why you're here. He's mistreating the dogs, right? Puppy mill? Miserable conditions? You know, he's been reported by every neighbor in south county."

Ozzie walked away toward the house.

"It's a social call."

"Aw, geez."

Donnie started the car and backed out of the driveway, not at all happy about doing so.

When Hatchett opened the door and saw the uniform, he froze for a moment, but quickly gathered himself.

"Can I help you?"

"Mr. Hatchett?"

Hatchett only nodded.

"I'd like to ask you a few questions, and see your backyard."

Colby stepped into the doorway. "Is this about our dog that's missing? She's awful sick and–"

Hatchett grabbed his arm, smiling, trying not to show the force he was using. "Didn't I tell you to go on about your chores?" He pushed Colby back into the living room and turned to Ozzie. "Why do you want to see the yard? We've done nothing wrong."

"No one is saying you have. But there are some questions . . ."

"And if I say no?"

Ozzie sighed and shuffled his foot.

"Mr. Hatchett, I can report that you're being uncooperative. I can get a warrant. I can take your last citation before Judge Williams, or I can report that you were very cooperative and everything's going to be just fine. Your choice."

Hatchett didn't like it, but he backed away from the door and ushered Ozzie in.

Across town, the orange van turned a corner and proceeded slowly down an oak-lined street, Sheldon and Livingston scanning every yard.

"We're never going to find her this way," said Sheldon. "We've been up and down every street in town six times."

"So what do you suggest Dr. 'D'? That we stop and ask a squirrel?"

"I suggest that we get outta this vehicle. Check under some of these houses. Prowl some back alleys. Go where a dog on the run would go."

Livingston was growing weary of Sheldon's dog psychology. "Oh, now you know where a dog on the run would go? Do you realize that we are two?! Just two! It would take days, weeks to check under every house in this town! How're we gonna do that? Huh? How?"

Sheldon was growing weary of Livingston's sarcasm. "Then stop and I'll ask a squirrel!" he grumbled, and turned his back to gaze out the window.

"Better yet, stop and I'll ask Lizard Tongue."

"What are you talking about?"

"The Tongue. He's right here. The other one too."

Benji and Lizard Tongue were trotting along beside the van, casting sideways glances up at Sheldon.

Livingston stretched to see out Sheldon's window. And, thankfully, Sheldon glanced up the road.

"Livingston!"

A huge delivery truck was backing out of a driveway right in front of them! Livingston slammed on the breaks and the van skidded to a stop, just inches from collision.

"I've had enough of this," Sheldon said. "I'm gonna do something productive. I'm either gonna catch me a Lizard Tongue or find out why the devil they won't leave us alone." He flung the door open and stepped out onto the sidewalk.

"Sheldon, get back in the car. We have work to do."

"And I'm about the business of doing it. See ya."

He slammed the door, feeling a new spirit and energy, then faced the two dogs who were standing not ten feet away. Rolling up his sleeves, he addressed them very politely, "Gentlemen, start your engines."

He took one step toward them, and they were off on a dead run, Sheldon in pursuit.

"Sheldon!" Livingston screamed to no avail. He breathed a huge unhappy sigh, shoved the van into reverse, parked, and joined the chase.

Only it wasn't a chase, really, because as Sheldon loped

around the first corner, the two dogs were waiting for him just up the sidewalk, and then they were off again. That happened every time Benji and Lizard Tongue got a bit too far ahead or turned a corner out of sight. They waited for him to catch up. It didn't take long for Sheldon to get it. He stopped at the entrance to the town park, breathing heavily, hands on his knees. He definitely needed to exercise more, he thought to himself.

The dogs were waiting, not twenty feet ahead of him. Livingston was huffing and puffing almost a block behind.

Sheldon eyed the two scraggly mutts, raised himself to his full height, which wasn't all that much, and took one step forward. Just one.

Benji took one step backward. Lizard Tongue watched, tongue dangling. *This is fun!*

Another step by Sheldon.

And another step backward by Benji. Lizard Tongue followed.

Sheldon loped out into an easy trot, and Benji turned and trotted off at the same pace. Lizard Tongue followed. He didn't get it, but he was having a good time.

Then, Sheldon stopped suddenly.

Benji turned back, sat down, and waited. Lizard Tongue followed his lead.

A tiny grin stretched across Sheldon's face.

"Dr. Doolittle indeed," he said out loud. And he broke into a fast jog. The dogs matched his speed, staying just ahead of him, and the threesome jogged off through the park, Livingston trying desperately to catch up.

Benji and Lizard Tongue turned the corner onto Burton Street, sprinted past the rusty wrought-iron gate at the old abandoned house, and trotted up the steps to the front door. They turned to wait for Sheldon, who wasn't far behind. The panting dogcatcher paused to catch his breath, and he couldn't help the big grin that covered his face. The old abandoned house where he had wanted to look in the first place! He was beginning to realize that he wasn't nearly as stupid as his partner wanted him to think. He trotted up to the porch and followed the dogs into the house. Livingston was just rounding the corner.

Sheldon broke into the foyer and tried to blink away the darkness. He spun around to a loud bark, and there they were. In the parlor. Benji and Lizard Tongue, standing just beyond Daisy, who appeared to be hanging on by a mere thread. Sheldon leaped across the room to the sick black dog and dropped to his knees, listening immediately to her lungs. He lifted her eyelid, then stroked her head lovingly. He looked up at Benji and their eyes locked for quite some time, each somehow understanding the other. Sheldon accepted the charge. He would take care of Benji's mom. And Benji knew he would.

"Sheldon! Are you in there?!" Livingston was screaming from outside, his footsteps clomping up onto the porch. Benji and Sheldon exchanged a last look, and Sheldon couldn't help himself when he gave a nod to this very special dog. Then Benji spun and dashed out through the kitchen, out of the house, Lizard Tongue right on his heels.

Sheldon rubbed Daisy head to tail. "It's okay, mama. You're gonna be okay now."

Livingston burst through the front door and appeared in the entrance to the parlor, jolting to a stop, mouth agape.

"I don't believe it."

"I'll take my told-you-so's later," Sheldon said. "We gotta get her to the clinic right now."

"But how did—"

Sheldon spun to Livingston, rising to new heights. He was in charge now and he wasn't going to fail. "*Now*, Livingston! Help me."

Livingston obeyed immediately. He hurried over and together they lifted Daisy from the floor. He gawked at Sheldon with a new respect, and awe.

22

Ozzie walked through the front door onto the porch and turned back to Hatchett. "I want to see it cleaned up under those cages, more shade for the dogs, an exercise area in place, and fresh water in every cage when I come back. Is that clear?"

Hatchett just wanted him gone. "Anything else?" he said dryly.

"I'll let you know after I've done a bit of research."

"On what?"

"Like I said, I'll let you know."

He turned and walked off the porch. Hatchett watched as the squad car backed out of the driveway, then he slammed the door. As soon as Hatchett was back in the house, Donnie Madison popped out of the shrubbery and climbed onto the porch. He withdrew his portable recorder and knocked on the door. It swung open and Colby appeared in the doorway. Donnie flashed a big toothy grin.

"Good afternoon. I'm Donnie Madison. WMUM. The

Voice of South County. We, of course, know why Officer Lewis was just here and I wondered if you would like to comment on his visit for our listeners."

He thrust the recorder at Colby, who stared at it for a moment, then grinned. He was just opening his mouth to speak when Hatchett jerked him out of the doorway, and the door slammed shut.

"I guess not," Donnie mumbled to himself.

He made one stop at his friend Zelda Pinkstrum's house, then raced back to the station just in time for his afternoon broadcast. You couldn't even really call it a station. There was nothing but an old wooden desk with a few antiquated pieces of equipment and a microphone. Through the window behind him, cows meandered in a barnyard.

"And the news of the day here in South County is the police visit to the Terrence Hatchett household. All on the q.t. of course, but your journalist was there on the scene and saw it happen. No comment from the Hatchetts, or the officer in charge, Sergeant Ozwald Lewis, but this from neighbor Zelda Pinkstrum."

Donnie pushed a button to start the tape.

Hatchett was alone in the kitchen, listening to Zelda on a small portable radio.

"I just say it's about time, 'cause everybody knows the awful way he treats those dogs in the backyard. They're just breeding machines is what they are. My sister Betty Lou down at the feed store says he buys the cheapest food and not nearly enough for a hundred dogs. That's what I heard! A hundred dogs! Of course, I haven't seen 'em to count 'em, mind you."

Zelda didn't get another word out of that little radio because Hatchett reached out and whacked it, sending it sailing across the kitchen, shattering into the far wall. The pieces fell onto the countertop in a heap, and Zelda was silenced.

Colby was in his fort, also listening to the broadcast. Merlin was perched on his shoulder, pacing back and forth. Donnie was talking again.

"It looks like headaches for the Hatchetts, and we thank Zelda for telling it like it is. The lines are open here for anyone else who has inside info." He issued the phone number, and then said, "Now a little bit of our song of the day, you guessed it, 'Man's Best Friend is not a Moose'."

Colby clicked off the radio and looked at Merlin.

"We gotta do something, Merlin."

Merlin paced.

"*I've* gotta do something," said Colby.

"*I'll be back*," squawked Merlin.

Colby looked at the bird, and nodded.

23

The doctor stripped away his sanitary mask and turned to the sink to wash his hands. Daisy lay on a stainless steel examination table under a bright white light with an IV taped to one leg. Miriam, Sheldon, Livingston, and Ozzie were huddled in the clinic doorway.

"She's dehydrated, and anemic, and infected from hookworms," the vet said. "I've started an IV and an antibiotic. I also think she might have a mammary tumor. Too much nursing. All that we can deal with, but the larger issue is she has pyometra."

"What's pyometra?" asked Miriam.

"Infected uterus. Overbreeding. It's a fast moving, awful condition and without immediate surgery, we'll lose her. I mean surgery *now*."

"Can you do it?"

The doctor nodded, and added, "But she has to be spayed

in the process. She'll never breed again."

Miriam sighed and turned to Ozzie.

"Can't do it, honey," he said. "Not without clearing it with Hatchett."

"Are you kidding? He wants to breed her to her last breath!"

"Don't you have a lawyer on your board?" Ozzie asked.

Miriam looked at Daisy and the sight of this very sick dog was stifling. She could not hold back the tears filling her eyes. "Can you hang around for a bit?" she asked the doctor.

"I'll be right here."

Her call to the lawyer did not bring good news. Sheldon, Livingston, and Ozzie waited patiently until Miriam put the phone down.

"If we operate without Hatchett's permission, he could sue us," she said.

"How can he sue us for saving her life?" Sheldon asked.

"The dog is his property. We can probably get him into court for abuse, but that takes time. Time we don't have."

There was a silence around the room. Finally, Ozzie spoke up.

"What are you going to do?"

Miriam was gazing off into space, thoughts churning. She reached for the phone, checked a number on her desk, punched it in, and waited. Her frustration at what she heard filled the room.

"I was hoping he wasn't home," she said.

"How do you know he's home," Sheldon asked.

She held up the phone. "It's busy."

Hatchett was screeching into the phone. "Lady, I don't care what you think. Or what the radio station thinks. My dogs are my business!" And he slammed the phone down.

It rang immediately. It had been ringing continuously since Donnie's broadcast. Hatchett snatched it off the receiver, and just listened. Finally, he said, "I do nothing of the sort! I love my dogs! Now stop calling here!"

Slam!

And, again, it rang instantly.

"I'm warning you people!" he shouted into the phone. "No, I have ten dogs. That's all! Ten!"

Slam!

Seething, he climbed out of his chair.

The phone rang again. He stared at it for a long moment, then paced back and forth across the room, near explosion. He finally dropped into a chair in the hallway and stared daggers at the ringing machine.

It continued to ring. And ring. And ring.

Miriam was holding the phone just away from her ear.

"You are my witnesses," she said to the group. "Seven . . . eight . . . nine . . . ten rings. That's it! We tried."

She replaced the phone onto the receiver and hit an intercom button.

"Dr. Garrett."

"At your service," the doctor replied.

"Proceed with the surgery. Save that dog's life. Please!"

"I'll do my best."

Miriam relaxed in her chair with a sigh. "My guess is that Hatchett will not want her back if she can't make puppies, so we'll find her a good home."

Ozzie frowned. He didn't feel it would end that neatly.

It was late in the day. Mr. Paul's market was closed, but the array of a dozen or so battered, rusty garbage cans in the back alley held the day's spoils, just waiting for two hungry heroes who had run all over town saving Benji's mom. Benji was balanced on top of a can, urging Lizard Tongue to join him. He nudged the lid of an adjacent can with his nose, the very tallest can in the bunch. The lid slid off and hit the ground with a clang, and then spun on itself like a top. Both dogs froze, and waited. But the market was empty. All remained quiet. And, now, the aroma of barbeque filled the air. Inside the tall can was the mother lode. Lizard Tongue couldn't resist, and he clambered aboard and tiptoed shakily from lid to lid, over to Benji's side.

Wow! Barbeque ribs! And chicken! And biscuits!

Benji leaned in, trying to reach the goodies. Lizard Tongue joined in the stretch. He was longer, maybe that would help. The smell of barbequed meat was thick down there in the can. They stretched further, and further. And suddenly their weight tipped the can. Just a bit. But quite enough for them to lose their grip and—

Whoops!

Two doggie tails vanished from sight into the depths of the tallest can in the bunch.

Now they were *way* down there . . . looking way *up*. Both were on hind legs, but even Lizard Tongue could not reach the rim. He jumped, and stretched. And accomplished nothing. He glanced at Benji, beginning to panic. *What now, dude?*

Benji began to jump against the side of the can, trying to tip it over. But this can was right in the middle of the bunch so there wasn't much tipping going on, just rocking back and forth. Violent rocking, as Lizard Tongue joined the effort. He let out a mournful *warf* that sounded more like the sad cry of a wolf. Benji kept jumping. And jumping.

As dusk settled around the Finch house, it was quiet and peaceful. But not happy. Finch sat at the edge of the porch, chin in hand, with growing certainty that he would never see his new friend again. The food bowl was next to him, overflowing with kibble. He nudged it a little closer to the edge of the porch. Easier to get to. Then he tidied the mound to make it neater.

And he waited.

The hoot of an owl woke him from a sound sleep. It was night, and he now held the food bowl in his lap, his arms wrapped around it as if it were Lizard Tongue himself. The old man scanned the woods beyond the lawn, and fell back asleep.

In the alley behind the market, the very tallest can continued to rock back and forth, the dogs now taking turns, one jumping while the other rested. It was hard work, but slowly and surely, the tallest can was pushing two other cans farther and farther away. Slowly and surely, the tall can was tipping farther and farther over.

Benji curled up in a ball on the bottom of the can, and Lizard Tongue took over. Jumping. And jumping.

A distant rooster crowed as the sun rose over the little white house in the meadow. Finch was still huddled against the porch rail, food bowl in his lap. He awoke with a start, then realized he was still alone. Sadly, he pulled himself up and walked inside. Almost as an afterthought, he returned and replaced the bowl on the porch. Why not?

The market had just opened for business when Benji's final jump sent the can next to theirs tumbling, and the very tallest can in the bunch clattered down onto its side. Benji and Lizard Tongue were gone in a flash, across the alley and around the corner, a mere instant before Mr. Paul came bursting through the back door of the market.

"What's going on out here?!" he screeched. But there was nothing to see except the mess.

24

Hatchett was nose-to-nose with Miriam, screaming right into her face!

"You what?!"

Miriam recoiled, pushing her chair back from the desk. Hatchet spun around and paced across the room. "Do you have any idea how rare that dog is?! And now she's worthless!"

"She would've died if we hadn't operated."

"I don't believe you people! You want to fix every dog in sight! But this time you overstepped the law, young lady! That dog belongs to me! You had no right to do what you did!"

"We had an obligation to save the dog's life if we could."

"The only obligation you had was to *me*!"

Behind Hatchett, through the glass wall into the reception area, Miriam saw Ozzie rush through the front door. He gestured, asking if he should come in, and Miriam nodded.

He opened the door behind Hatchett.

"Nancy called. Is everything okay?"

"No, everything is not okay," Hatchett said angrily.

"We tried to reach you. You weren't home," Miriam said to Hatchett.

"That was my prize breeder!"

Ozzie gave him a stern look. "I believe you told an Animal Control officer that you rarely bred her."

Ooops.

"Well, she was—"

"She was being way overbred," said Miriam. "That's why she was so sick."

There was a moment of silence as Hatchett evaluated his position. Miriam broke the quiet, hoping to end it.

"I assume that since she can no longer have puppies, you will have no further need for her. We'll find her a good home."

Hatchett spun toward her. "Not on your life! She's coming home with me!"

"Why?" quizzed Ozzie, trying to persuade reasonably. "You have no use for her."

Hatchett marched over to Miriam's desk and leaned down, face-to-face, hands plopped right on his own file folder. Ozzie eased in closer, just in case.

"Oh, yes, I do have a use for her," Hatchett said. "She's my evidence when I take you people to court! Now get me my dog!"

Miriam sank into her chair. Ozzie slid behind her and put a hand on her shoulder. She knew in her heart that returning the dog to Hatchett was not the right thing to do. She didn't want to reach for the intercom, but after a long moment, she did.

Benji walked Lizard Tongue out of the woods to the edge of Finch's lawn, then stopped. Lizard Tongue walked on for a moment before turning back. The two dogs gazed at each other for quite some time, neither seeming to move a muscle. They had been through a lot together.

Up at the house, Finch was standing just inside the screen door, watching, wondering how long these two had been friends, and just what they had been up to. It seemed clear that they cared for each other. He watched Lizard Tongue glance toward the house, then back to Benji. Was he making a decision? To go or to stay?

Benji woofed. A small, soft woof. Lizard Tongue returned it, but even small, it still came out *warf.* He walked over and licked Benji in the face. Just once. Then Benji turned and walked off toward the woods. Lizard Tongue watched him for a long moment. *Why did it have to be this way?* But, somehow, at some level, he knew that it did. He turned and trotted slowly toward the house.

Finch met him at the edge of the porch with a big hug.

"Whoa!" He chuckled, sniffing his coat. "Did you spend the night in a garbage can?"

Lizard Tongue licked him in the face, and the old man chuckled again and took his new friend into the house.

Benji was watching from the edge of the woods. He wasn't sure where he'd go next, but he turned to leave.

The huge net came out of nowhere! Benji panicked as it fell around him. Just as quickly, the two dogcatchers appeared. He tried to leap away as Sheldon bent over him, but he was tangled! Trapped! Sheldon's hand found his head and scratched it caringly.

"Calm down. It's gonna be okay. I promise."

He removed the net and held Benji close to his chest.

"Go ahead. Tell him," said Livingston. "You can talk to these guys."

Sheldon stood and walked off toward the little bridge over the stream.

"Nah, no need to get his hopes up."

Livingston gathered up the net and followed.

"I think you should tell him. This could be a big deal."

"No," said Sheldon. "I don't think so."

"Why not? He might not want any part of it. A dog should be able to make his own decisions on stuff like this."

Sheldon turned to face Livingston. "And what if you build up his hopes for nothing. Then what? You have no compassion." He walked on.

"Whaddaya mean 'build up his hopes for nothing'? It's not gonna be for nothing. Just look at that face!"

The newspaper hit the coffee table with a force. A huge picture of Benji covered the page, with a bold headline that read: MOVIE PRODUCER SAYS LOCAL STRAY COULD BE A STAR! Under that was the question: COULD THIS BE THE NEW BENJI?

Hatchett was screaming at Colby. "Look at that! It's the mutt you've been keeping out in the woods, ain't it?!"

Colby dropped to the floor to read the article. *How cool!*

Claire was drawn into the room by the screaming. She saw the newspaper and stopped to read it over Colby's shoulder.

"Well ain't it?" Hatchett persisted. "That's *our* dog they're trying to run off with! *Our* dog!"

Colby couldn't believe his ears. "*Our* dog? Even if it's the same dog, he's not *our* dog! You left that puppy to die."

"Not anymore! They're gonna pay if they think they're gonna make our dog a star! Pay big! Those animal people owe me!" He pushed Colby toward the stairs to his bedroom.

"Go put on a decent shirt. We're going down there to claim our dog."

Colby paused at the doorway.

"I don't want to go."

"What you want doesn't matter to me. You're going. And you're going to tell 'em it's your dog. It'll play better coming from a kid."

He turned to face Claire. "You're going, too. We're going down there as a family to claim our dog. Or our reward."

Claire shook her head. "I'm not going."

Hatchett stepped closer, glaring at her. She stood her ground, and he got so close she could smell his foul breath.

"Oh, yes, you are," he said.

25

Benji was sprawled on Miriam's desk, watching, listening. Sensing that important stuff was going on here.

The room was full of people, and Miriam was pacing and talking. "We picked him up three days ago. Legally, he now belongs to Animal Control, to do with as we feel best."

Sheldon, Livingston, and Ozzie were in the room. But she was speaking to a new face—the movie producer who was searching through animal shelters across the country for the new Benji. The minute Sheldon had read about the search, he had made a phone call. He was convinced that this dog who had led him all the way across town to the old house not only looked like Benji, but was special enough to be everything Benji had ever been. But that wasn't the issue at the moment.

"You don't understand," the producer said. "The legal question doesn't matter."

Mini-blinds covered the glass wall between Miriam's office and the reception room. The producer walked over and pulled the string, just enough to see through. The Hatchett family was sitting on a bench across the room, Hatchett in a rumpled coat and tie. Daisy, still in her surgical bandages, sat at Colby's feet. The producer pointed to Benji.

"If this dog belongs to that young boy out there, we're not taking him away. We're not. I don't care what the law says."

Benji was stretching to see into the next room. He recognized Daisy and couldn't help the tail wag. Miriam scratched him on the head.

"This dog has been on the streets for a long time. Our guys have seen him. And that man out there is a bad person. He lies. He mistreats dogs. That black one almost died because of him!"

"And you should know this," Sheldon chimed in. "This dog is the reason that dog out there is still alive. He led us right to her."

"He did," nodded Livingston, "right to her."

The producer walked over to Benji and scratched him behind an ear. Their eyes locked for a moment, the producer grappling with the notion that this was one bright dog he might be giving up. He glanced out at Colby, who was rubbing Daisy lovingly on the head. She reached up and licked his hand.

"There's no way you'll convince me that kid out there is gonna come in here and lie. If it's his dog, it stays his dog."

Miriam looked at Ozzie and sighed openly. "Might as well bring 'em in," she said.

Ozzie leaned out the door. "You can come in now."

Colby entered first with Daisy. Hatchett followed and stood close behind him. Claire eased away into a nearby corner. The room was quiet and filled with tension.

The producer lifted Benji off the desk and placed him on the floor. The floppy-eared mutt with the big brown eyes wanted to run to Daisy, or Colby, but the anxiety in the room held him in place. He glanced from one to the other. The producer faced the Hatchetts. Colby had not reacted to Benji at all, hadn't even looked at him. His eyes were fixed on the producer. Hatchett shoved him forward.

"Well, go on. Tell 'em. Tell 'em it's your dog."

"Hi, son," said the producer. "What's your name?"

"Colby."

"Colby, I understand this dog has been on the streets for some time. How will you know if it's your dog?"

"I'll know," Colby said. He looked down at Daisy. "She'll know."

Hatchett shoved him again. "Go on."

Colby took the rope off Daisy and turned her loose. She and Benji gazed at each other, then she limped over and licked him in the face. Colby followed, and dropped to his knees to scratch Benji on the head. He lifted his friend's chin until their eyes met. Benji reached out and licked him on the nose.

"Well, go ahead, tell 'em!" Hatchett said, becoming agitated. "Tell 'em it's your dog!"

Colby glanced over his shoulder at Hatchett, who nodded and gestured for him to get it done. He found Claire in the corner, and she could have sworn she saw the slightest of smiles, but maybe not. Then, Colby turned to the producer.

"Sorry, mister. There must be some mistake. This is not my dog."

Silence. This was not the answer anyone in the room expected.

Claire bit her lip, unable to resist the smile that was clearly stretching across her face. Hatchett bellowed, "What do you mean it's not your dog?! It most definitely is your dog!" He leaped across the room, jerked Colby off the floor, and shook him hard. Ozzie was on him before he could blink, locking Hatchett's arm behind his back.

"Just calm yourself down, Mr. Hatchett."

"Get your hands off me!"

Hatchett tried to wrestle away, and yelped in pain as Ozzie applied twist to his arm.

"Either you calm down or you'll be spending the rest of the day in jail!"

Ozzie moved him out into the reception room, closing the door behind him. He sat Hatchett down on the bench against the far wall, and slowly released his grip. Hatchett was steaming, but knew better than to cause any more trouble.

"If I were you I would sit here nice and quiet and not as much as move a muscle to go back in there."

Ozzie strolled across the room, nodded to Nancy behind the reception desk, and borrowed her phone. He turned to keep an eye on Hatchett, who was fixed on what was going on behind the glass in Miriam's office. The producer was speaking to Colby, but Hatchett could hear none of what was being said. When Ozzie finished his call, he returned to the office, raising the mini-blinds all the way up so he would have an unobstructed view of Hatchett.

Miriam had joined the conversation with Colby and appeared to be concerned about whatever they were talking about. She looked up at Hatchett, who was growing very uneasy. He shifted in his seat, and glanced at the front door, clearly worried about where this was headed.

The producer spoke again to Colby, then Miriam asked the boy a question. And quite suddenly everyone in the room looked at Claire. She seemed to gasp and glanced nervously at Hatchett. He fired off a warning look.

Ozzie approached her and asked a question. Claire shook her head no. He asked again, and waited, and finally she nodded. He reached up and gently pushed back a wave of hair to reveal a nasty bruise on her forehead.

All heads spun to Hatchett. He leaped for the front door and vanished into the bright sunlight outside.

"Ozzie! He's getting away!" Miriam screeched.

Ozzie had his back to the door. He smiled and shook his

head, and then turned to see two uniformed police officers dragging Hatchett back through the doorway.

"I suspect the judge will be sending him to a nice place where he'll get some help. And, in the meantime, he won't be around to do anymore harm to you guys, or your dogs."

The producer turned to Colby. "So, this is your dog after all."

Colby gestured to Daisy. "No, sir. It's *her* dog."

The producer took a long look at Benji, absorbed in his big brown eyes, and the notion that if the tales were true, this might well be the brightest dog he'd ever met. He reached down and scratched Benji behind an ear.

"Well, son, the last thing we want to do is take your dog away."

Colby blinked as the words sank in.

"No!" he suddenly blurted. "No, you've got it all wrong!"

He was searching for words.

"I wouldn't do anything in the world to stop him from becoming Benji!" He pulled Benji close to him. "This dog has had such a hard life."

He had to pause for a moment to wipe the moisture from his eyes.

"I mean, a really hard life. He deserves something good. He deserves to be famous. Please, oh please, mister. Let him be in your movie. Please!"

The producer didn't know what to say. He looked to

Miriam for help. Claire was sniffing back tears, and Miriam was reaching for a tissue herself.

"Please!" Colby pleaded. "I love him very much, but if you think he could be a star . . ."

There was silence in the room. Everybody waited.

Finally the producer said, "Looks to me like he already is." Then, he reached into a pocket and withdrew a bright red collar with a familiar gold disc dangling from it on which was engraved the word *Benji*.

He handed the collar to Colby.

Colby gazed at it, his eyes filling and overflowing. How could he have known when he named this dog Benji, that he would really become Benji? The *real* Benji! Sniffling and wiping, he snapped the collar around Benji's neck. Colby was beaming when he looked up and found the producer, who had walked across the room to retrieve a tissue for himself.

"Just one thing," Colby said.

The producer turned.

"If, maybe, I could just come and visit him every once in a while?"

The producer smiled.

"I think we can fix it so you can come visit him any time you want. How about that?"

Claire began to sob outright. Even Sheldon was fighting it.

Colby pulled Benji close and gave him a big, big hug, wondering how he could feel so happy and so sad all at the same time. Benji reached up and gave him an affectionate lick on the face.

It was the first kiss Colby had ever had from a real movie star.

Epilogue

A photograph of Benji and Colby appeared on the front page of the local newspaper the next day. Finch recognized the dog immediately. He called Lizard Tongue over and showed it to him.

"Looks to me like it's time to call in the favors."

Sheldon had already thought of it. Even suggested it to the producer. And it really wasn't a bad idea. A movie with Benji *and* Lizard Tongue!

"And, maybe a bird," said Sheldon.

Maybe, someday.

Author's Note

The new Benji was adopted from the Humane Society of South Mississippi in the city of Gulfport. Lizard Tongue was adopted from the Animal Care and Control shelter in South Chicago. We, of course, don't know what their real story was prior to adoption . . . but it could've been the story you've just read.

Woof.

Benji has formed the Benji's Buddies Foundation with a mission to raise the levels of adoptions in animal shelters significantly across the country. For more information go to: **www.BenjiBuddiesFoundation.com**

For more information about *Benji*, go to: **www.Benji.info**

To adopt a pet anywhere within the continental United States, go to: **www.Pets911.com**